LOVE WILL FIND A WAY

JULIE BENTZ

Copyright © 2020 Julie Bentz
All rights reserved.

Paperback: 978-1-64746-439-4
Hardback: 978-1-64746-440-0
Ebook: 978-1-64746-441-7
Library of Congress Control Number: 2020915089

This book is dedicated to my four sons:

Donovan

Damien

Austin

Logan

Always follow your hearts and your dreams.

PART ONE
Annie

CHAPTER 1

The late September sun resembled a brilliant gemstone in the bright blue sky high above the schoolhouse, the focal point of the tiny farming community of Gregory. It was a Tuesday afternoon, and a cluster of children scrambled down the steps of the rickety old building and scattered in every direction. Except for Annie Allister and her best friend, Margaret Wilson. They were two of the older students, and they descended slowly down the steps as proper young ladies should.

As they left the schoolyard behind them, Annie stopped short. "Look. Up ahead." She extended a long, dainty finger in the direction she wanted her friend to look. The object of Annie's fascination was an ordinary wagon occupied by unfamiliar faces.

Margaret clapped her hands together. "A new family in town. How exciting." Her voice became shrill as she spoke the last word, and Annie knew her friend sugar-coated her excitement with sarcasm. Margaret rarely expressed excitement over changes in the community.

But Annie herself was instantly intrigued. New families didn't often move into Gregory. It was far too small for anyone to make a living. They had a restaurant, post office, feed mill, and of course the mercantile, but these businesses already had their owners running them, and they didn't need to hire anyone else. She felt they needed to investigate, so the two young ladies made their way closer to the wagon, never taking their eyes from it.

The driver of the wagon was nowhere in sight, but a small, pretty woman and two young children peeked through the canvas in the back. A young man sat at the head of the wagon holding the team. As Annie and Margaret approached, he glanced their way. He tipped his hat at them and said, "Howdy, ladies."

The two friends looked at each other and tried to stifle giggles as they walked past him, continuing on their way home. Annie couldn't help but look over her shoulder again and again at him. "Isn't he handsome?"

"I'll admit he is rather good-looking, but he also looks much older than us." A scowl formed on Margaret's lips. Annie shook her head. Margaret was always the skeptic. Her thoughts never extended beyond the present moment. She would rather sew than give any thought to boys.

"That doesn't matter," Annie brushed off the negative comment, and her mischievous eyes lit up as an idea entered her brain. She laid a finger on her chin and, as if speaking to no one in particular, asked, "I wonder if he would be interested in escorting me to the Fall Social?"

Margaret appeared shocked. "Annie Allister," she scolded, "you put that thought right out of your head. There are plenty of boys your own age who would be delighted to ask you. I know that for a fact. Besides, you don't even know him."

Growing more irritated with Margaret's constant skepticism, Annie said, "I realize that, Margaret, but I want to go with him." Sometimes she could be such a bore. And then, in a nasty tone, she added, "And you sound like my mother." But Margaret ignored that remark and shook her head. Annie quickly realized how dumb that had sounded. Margaret got on quite well with Mama.

The two girls continued walking. It was nice that they lived so close to each other. That was how they had become friends in the first place, when they were only babies, and now that they were older, they were able to walk to and from school together. In fact, their mothers joked they were like twins. Their farms were located at the very foot of The Hill, along with three other farms, all of which could be seen at the very top. It was a breathtaking view with trees dotting the distant landscape.

The Hill, although it was nothing more than a hill, was a well-known landmark to the residents of Gregory. The town itself sat on one side of it, and scaling up the steep side of it brought you to the top where a cluster of farms could be seen. It was almost like a whole other town. The older residents referred to it as the dividing line between the businesses and the families.

When the girls reached the top, they sat down in the tall weeds to catch their breath before finishing their journey. "It has been so nice out lately," Margaret commented nonchalantly, leaning back on her elbows to allow the warm sun to envelope her. She hoped to change the subject they had discussed previously.

Annie nodded her head absently and said nothing. Her mind traveled someplace else, and her friend noticed immediately. Margaret sighed deeply. "Well, I can see that you are not interested in having any sort of meaningful conversation with me right now, so I had best get home and help my ma with the supper." She stood up, and it didn't take long for Annie to follow suit.

"Oh, I had best move it too. I can already see Beth startin' towards the barn." She brushed the grass off the backside of her dress.

"Yeah," Margaret agreed, "I know how upset your little sister can get when you skip out on your share of the chores."

Annie smiled and nodded her head. Margaret knew her family too well. "I'll see you tomorrow in school. 'Bye." Margaret waved, and the girls parted in separate directions.

The minute Annie stepped foot in the yard, Pup ran to meet her, jumping up and playfully wagging his tail. As much as she loved him, Annie had no time to give to the family pet. Already late, she tossed her school books carelessly down by the fence post and headed for the barn to see how far her sister had gotten with the afternoon chores.

It took only one glance at Beth's beautiful young face to know something was going on. Instead of her usual remark about Annie being late, Beth said nothing. She was too busy raking up the hay the horses had scattered around. Annie supposed she was simply angry at having to start by herself, so she ignored Beth's flippant attitude and grabbed the full pail of chicken feed. As she made her way toward the coop, Beth looked up from the raking she was doing and flashed her sister an irritated glare. "It certainly took you long enough to show up and help. Pa expects us to finish up quickly and then get right inside to help Mama with supper."

Annie wondered what was going on as she lightly tossed some feed to the chickens. Pa usually wasn't so strict about things. Sometimes, he would allow his two daughters to horse around during their chores as long as they were done properly. And once, Annie could even remember his carefree nature exposing itself when he joined them rolling around in the hay.

But today was different, and Annie was anxious to find out why. She went about setting out saucers of milk for the cats, and suddenly, her mind went back to the young man she had seen earlier. He was mighty handsome. She wondered what his name was and where he and his family came from.

"Are you almost done?" Beth's voice cut through her thoughts.

"Yes," Annie called out. Honestly, Beth could be such a pain sometimes. She was only twelve, but she couldn't wait to be like her big sister. She would sometimes hang around when Margaret was visiting, which annoyed Annie. But, as she watched Beth make her way up to the house, she had to admit her baby sister was much better at doing her chores than Annie herself was.

Annie wiped her hands on the front of her skirt before remembering Mama would have a fit if she saw that. She ran to catch up to Beth so they could walk to the house together.

The minute they opened the door, Annie smelled the fragrant daisies Mama had picked. She always had an assortment of flowers in the middle of the table. They went to Mama and gave her a hug and a kiss on the cheek. "Hi, Mama," they greeted in unison.

Mama wore her usual sunny smile and flushed cheeks from a hard day of work, and her voice was full of authority as she addressed her daughters. She flung aprons in their direction and hurled out one command after another. "Put these on. Beth, peel some potatoes. Annie, start a cake for dessert. Your pa wants supper early tonight; he has some company coming afterwards."

Again, Annie's curiosity was piqued. She always needed to know what was going on. "Who's coming, Mama?"

"Someone who is interested in helping your pa rebuild the barn," she answered, not looking up from her work.

That wasn't a satisfying answer for Annie, but she knew better than to argue with her mother, and besides, the three women had a meal to prepare. And they did it successfully. Pa was delighted with his heaping plate of fried chicken, mashed potatoes, corn bread, and Annie's chocolate cake. "You ladies never fail," he praised. Pa always said he was the luckiest man in the country to have three such fine women.

It didn't take long for Annie to notice Pa's mood. He seemed happier than usual, and Annie figured she knew why. If the gentleman who was coming agreed to help Pa rebuild the barn, Pa would have more time to devote to all the other repairs around the farm that desperately needed his attention.

The Allister family ate their meal in a rare silence. Normally, they each discussed how their day had gone, but tonight, there wasn't time for that. They had to clear the table to prepare for the arrival of their company.

After finishing their chores, Annie became restless and thought the mystery man would never show up, but her long wait by the window finally came to an end when she noticed a wagon approaching from the very top of The Hill. "Whoever you're waiting for, Pa, is coming," Annie announced, apparently too loudly because Mama scolded.

"Annie Elizabeth Allister," her voice bellowed out. "There is no need to shout. Now, I expect you to be on your best behavior when Mr. Montgomery is here."

Annie felt her cheeks redden. She wasn't aware that she had shouted, but she knew when her mother used her full name, she meant business. Annie decided she would behave from this point on, because if she didn't, she would likely be sent to her room she shared with Beth. Then, she would miss everything.

Finally, there was a knock on the door, and Pa rose from his chair to answer it. Annie eyed him carefully and discovered the man was similar to Pa. He dressed the same and appeared to be the same age as well.

His hair was the color of sand, and he had a beard to match.

Annie sighed and turned away from the door, feeling let down. She went to the kitchen and put the coffee on the stove. The visitor she was hoping for was someone of importance who wore expensive clothing and came from an exotic place. Instead, he turned out to be an ordinary, hard-working man like her pa. But the more she thought of it, the more she came to realize that no one like the person she envisioned would be interested in building a barn.

Annie took some coffee cups out of the cabinet and turned to the table to set the cups down and start serving coffee. And then, as if by magic, the handsome young gentleman she had seen earlier appeared in the doorway behind Pa's guest.

Pa ushered them both in and then began introductions. "This is my beautiful wife, Lillian, my youngest daughter, Beth, and this is Annie." He pointed to each as he went.

Next, it was the stranger's turn. "Well, it's nice to meet y'all. I'm John Montgomery, and this is my brother, Will. We just moved here yesterday from out west. I need some work real bad. Me and the wife have two feisty boys to feed." He smiled proudly when mentioning his children. Then, he pointed his thumb at Will. "Will here said he'd be willin' to work too. And just last night, a fine feller in town said you needed some help puttin' up a barn." He sucked in a deep breath after rattling all of those sentences together.

"Well, you two gentlemen have yourselves a seat, and we'll get acquainted," Pa said. The two men sat down, and Annie served them all some hot, steaming coffee as Pa began explaining to the Montgomery men why the old barn needed fixing in the first place.

Annie shuddered as she recalled the horrible ordeal. It had been the hottest, stickiest night last summer, and it was obvious with one look at the sky that they were in for a storm. Halfway through the night, Pa fiercely shook his two daughters awake. Annie knew in an instant a vicious twister was coming. It sounded as though a gigantic stampede of buffalo was about to trample their tiny farmhouse. The Allister family bolted out of the house and into the root cellar, desperately clinging to each other in the threatening winds. Annie was quite certain she felt the ground shaking from nature's wrath. The family had made it to safety, but the farm took quite a beating. Mama's garden was completely destroyed as were Pa's crops and the barn, of course. Even the innocent little outhouse had been brutally overturned.

Annie's daydreaming came to a halt when she heard the final part of the men's conversation. "I will be working with old Mr. Jones east of town, helping him plant his crops and such," John explained, "but as I said, Will is looking for work too."

"Y-yes, sir," Will stammered. "I would be happy to take the job—if you'll have me."

Pa's jolly laugh rang out. "Well then, Will Montgomery, you have it. Welcome aboard." The two men shook hands to finalize the deal.

And all the while, Annie felt a strange tingling feeling deep within her. She instantly recognized it as a crush. She knew because she had had a crush on Robert Manning just last year. He and his family lived right down the road from the Allister's until Robert's father had found work in the big city, causing the family to move away. Now, she had these same feelings for Will. She was glad he had taken the job.

CHAPTER 2

The next morning's sun shone on Annie's sleeping face, warming her cheeks and urging her to wake up. Her tired eyelids were stubborn, though, and Annie had to force them open. Today was Saturday, Will's first day on the job, and she wasn't about to miss a minute of this day by lying around in bed. She whipped the blankets off her body and stood up, stretching her arms high above her head. *Yes, today will be a lovely day*, she thought as she stole a quick glance out the window.

Annie knew her other family members were awake by now because she heard them scuffling about and speaking in hushed tones in the kitchen. Her sharp nose smelled the comforting breakfast of eggs and bacon, and she dressed hurriedly. She carelessly brushed her flowing brown hair before joining the family.

Her mother cast her a look of surprise when she entered the kitchen. "You're up early," she observed. Then, grinning mischievously, she said, "And it isn't even noon yet."

Annie ignored the sarcastic remark and sat down at the table next to Beth. "I have a full day planned," she replied matter-of-factly.

"Oh? And just exactly what will you be doing?" Beth inquired, not quite believing her big sister.

Annie glared at her. Sometimes she was so nosy. "For your information, I promised Mrs. Jacobs I would help keep an eye on her kids while she did some sewing." And as if that hadn't sounded grown up enough, she added, "She even offered to pay me." Nancy Jacobs and her husband, Roy, lived two miles away from the Allisters'. They had seven young children, which made it challenging for Nancy to complete her daily tasks. Whenever Annie walked by the Jacobs' farm, she saw Nancy hanging out an enormous amount of wash. She knew Nancy could use any amount of help, and Annie was glad to offer it. She always tried refusing payment, but both Mr. and Mrs. Jacobs wouldn't hear of it.

Mama's face was glowing. "I am so proud of you, Annie. You are becoming such a responsible young woman."

Annie was stunned. She wasn't aware that her mother thought of her as a grown woman. But it was about time. After all, she was sixteen years old. It annoyed her that most people still thought of her as a child. Mama's remark suddenly gave Annie a new confidence in herself. It made her more determined than ever to show the world she was a responsible adult instead of a child.

After slipping on her calico bonnet, Annie began her journey to the Jacobs' farm. She walked straight and tall, keeping in mind her mother's recent remark.

CHAPTER 3

It was early afternoon by the time Annie was through with helping Mrs. Jacobs, and by then, thick, gray clouds cluttered the sky. Annie shivered as she noticed the hint of coolness in the air. She guessed it would probably rain.

As Margaret's farm came into view, Annie decided to swing by for a visit as she had promised. She was tired but didn't mind because she always felt at home there. Chickens scooted out of the way as she walked up to the door and knocked loudly.

Not surprisingly, Margaret's mother answered the door, and when she saw Annie, a broad smile spread across her plump face. She pretended to be shocked and slapped her hand to her cheek. "Why, Annie Allister, whatever are you doing here?" She chuckled at her own silliness as she stepped aside to let Annie enter her cozy home. "Come on in, dear."

"Thank you," Annie said graciously. She had a great deal of respect for the Wilson family. They were like a second family to her. She recalled many times when Mama and Pa would take trips together when she and Beth were younger, and Margaret's ma was always the first to invite the two girls to stay with them. And of course, Annie always enjoyed being there because she felt loved and cared for by Margaret's family, despite the fact that they had seven children.

"Margaret is in her room. Jest go on up," Mrs. Wilson told Annie, although Annie already knew where to find her friend.

Annie climbed the steep ladder to the cozy little loft. She expected a warm welcome from her best friend, but what she saw frightened her for a moment.

Margaret lay face down on her bed, crying.

"Margaret," Annie's voice caught on a sob, "what's wrong?"

Margaret looked up at her closest friend. She sniffled a few times, then sat up and reached for a handkerchief. Her dress was rumpled, and her face was tear-stained. She blew her nose and then began her tale. "I talked to Joey today. Remember how me and you were talking about asking the boys to the dance instead of waiting for them to do it?"

Annie nodded. Unfortunately, she knew where this was leading.

"Well," Margaret continued, "I ran into him this morning in town while running errands for my ma. And Annie, I did it. I don't know how, but I found the courage, and I asked him." Her face darkened then.

"He said he already had a date. With Tammy Allen, of all people." She scrunched her nose in distaste.

Margaret burst into another round of tears and sobs. Annie took her hand. She wanted desperately to comfort her dear friend. "Oh, Margaret, I am so sorry." And she truly was. Margaret had had a crush on Joey for four years, and he knew it, and he visibly enjoyed her affections. If Margaret shared her lunch with him at school, he would carry her books home for her. He appeared interested in her at certain times, yet at others, he acted as though she never existed.

Annie fumed inside. She knew that boys were impossible, but Joey would choose Tammy, wouldn't he? She was, after all, the envy of every girl in town. Not only was she pretty and had all the boys' tongues wagging at all times, but she was also the banker's daughter, which meant she wore fancy clothes that only added to her striking beauty. It also helped that she lived in the fanciest home in the center of Gregory.

Well, Annie decided with determination, *I will see to it that dear Margaret is smiling again in no time.*

"Margaret," she began gently, "I will help you find another date. You may not believe this, but just last week, Carl Davis was asking about you."

That seemed to perk her right up. "He was?"

"Yes, he was." Annie smiled. "So, please don't let Joey upset you. He's not worth it."

Margaret blew her nose one last time. "Well, Carl would be my next choice for a date. But I don't know him that well. We've never really talked."

"Well, I've known him since he was in diapers." Annie chuckled. "Our mothers were friends when they were kids."

Margaret was grateful to her friend. "You sure know how to lift my spirits, Annie."

Annie smiled happily and threw her arm around her friend's shoulders. "Well, you know me. I'm always glad to help." Then, she thought of something. "Hey, did you still want to come over for supper? Mama is expecting you."

"Oh, of course. I would have to be a fool to pass up your mother's pot roast and cornbread." The girls laughed at that remark and went to the kitchen where Mrs. Wilson prepared her family's meal.

"Ma, I'm going over to Annie's for supper. Remember? I told you about it yesterday."

"Oh yes, darling," her mother replied. "Be sure to mind your manners."

Margaret rolled her eyes. "I'm not a child anymore, Ma."

Her mother smiled and nodded with understanding. She kissed her daughter's cheek, and the two girls hurried out the door.

The sky was a deep gray, and light rain pelted their faces the minute they stepped foot outside. They made their way across the thin, barely visible road that led to Annie's place. As they approached the farm, Annie came to an abrupt stop and clutched Margaret's arm.

"Ouch," Margaret cried out in pain. "What did you do that for?" she demanded.

Annie pointed and announced in a childish sing-song voice, "Look who's at my house."

They saw Annie's pa and Will standing by the shed gathering their supplies to begin working on the barn.

"This is perfect," she said as she whirled around to face Margaret. "I have been hoping to get to know him. This gives me the perfect opportunity."

Margaret shook her head, and the two girls entered the yard. They paid no attention to Pup's pleas for attention as they hurried to the barn.

Right before entering, Annie told Margaret, "Let's hurry up with the chores so we have more time for other things."

Annie pulled the sturdy door of the barn open and nearly collided with Beth, who wore a distasteful expression on her adolescent face. Annie knew it meant she was furious at her for once again being late for chores, but this time, she didn't care.

She grabbed the pail of chicken feed while Margaret began sweeping out the stalls. Annie had never worked harder or faster in her life. But she knew the sooner she finished, the more time she would have to talk to Will.

The girls finished their chores and then went over to the other side of the barn, the side with no roof. She looked up and smiled at the two men. "Hi, Pa, how's the work coming along?"

"Oh, just fine and dandy, precious," he answered. "Do you have all your chores done?"

Annie was embarrassed her father had used that term in front of Will. It was fine when they were alone but not in front of others. "Yes," she replied obediently. Then, she turned her attention on Will. "Hi, Will."

Will didn't miss a beat. "Well, hello there, um, precious? Was that your name?" He and Pa both chuckled at his joke.

Now, Annie was really embarrassed. But she was still determined to become more than friends with the dashing William Montgomery.

CHAPTER 4

"It sure was nice of your ma to let us sit and enjoy ourselves instead of helping with supper," Margaret said. The two girls were in Annie's room lying on the bed, swinging their legs in the air, chatting about nothing in particular.

"Well, Ma knows it's important for me and Beth to spend time with our friends. Besides, she always treats her guests right." She rolled off the bed and went over to the window. She gazed out at the men, who were discussing the work Will would be expected to do. She couldn't get Will off her mind.

A second later, Margaret crawled off the bed as well and went over to Annie's rickety little wooden table that held all her treasures. Carefully, she ran her fingertips over them, marveling at their beauty.

Picking one up, she asked, "Where did you get this one? It's so pretty."

"Huh?" Annie hadn't heard a word. She was too busy watching Will walk through the yard with Pa.

Margaret walked over to Annie and shoved the corn kernel necklace right in front of Annie's eyes. "I asked you where you got this. I haven't seen it before."

"Oh, uh, Beth made it for me last Christmas," Annie answered mechanically. Margaret pursed her lips as Annie continued. "I wish it wasn't raining. I would rather be outside. Watching him." She sighed. "Oh well, there will be other days." Her eyes lit up. "Just think, Margaret, he will be here almost every day helping my pa. I'll have so many chances to talk to him."

Margaret looked doubtful. "You'll probably chicken out."

"I will not!" Annie shot back. She wasn't sure if she was trying to convince Margaret or herself.

Margaret shrugged. "That's very brave of you. But you won't catch me waltzing up to Carl and begging him to be my date. I don't have that confidence like you do."

Annie completely understood. Margaret was painfully shy with most people, especially the ones she didn't know very well. She rarely even raised her hand in school, even if she knew the answer to the teacher's question.

"I will convince Carl to ask you to the Fall Social," Annie reminded her. "I promised you I would, and I will. Besides," she added, "it shouldn't be too hard to do. It sounds like Carl already had the same idea."

Margaret blushed when she heard that. "Oh, Annie, I don't know about that. I mean, I am pretty ordinary."

Annie snorted. "Now quit selling yourself short, Ms. Wilson. You are very beautiful, and I think you know it."

And she was. Margaret's long, golden hair glistened against the brightness of the sun, and her narrow eyes were a deep blue, and they went well with her full lips. She had plenty of young gentlemen interested in her, even if she didn't know it yet.

Annie wagged a finger in Margaret's face. "Mark my words. You and I will have the best-looking escorts at the Fall Social."

They giggled together, then retreated from the bedroom as Mrs. Allister's stern voice called them to supper. The girls sat down beside each other at the beautifully set table. Annie noticed right away that something was going on because Mama had used her delicate lace tablecloth, and she had set out an arrangement of wild flowers Beth had picked earlier.

But what really grabbed Annie's attention was the fine china at each setting. Annie was confused. She knew Mama only used her special dishes for company. Indeed, they had company. Margaret was here, but she had eaten here many times, and Mama had never gone to this trouble before.

Just then, the thick door swung open, and there stood Pa.

And Will.

Of course, Annie thought. She could have kicked herself for not using her head. Mama always fed the helping hands. Regretfully, she wished she had sat across from Margaret instead of beside her in hopes of having Will sit beside her. Annie could hardly contain herself. She wanted to scream with delight, but instead, she elbowed Margaret and looked at her mischievously.

Will took the only available seat left, which was beside Beth, and spoke to Mama. "Thank you for inviting me to share this meal with your family, Mrs. Allister. It looks real good."

Once again, Annie's heart fluttered with admiration. He was such a polite young man. But Mama brushed away his kind words with her hand. "Nonsense. Visitors are always welcome in our home."

"Thank you, ma'am," he repeated. They passed the platters and bowls full of succulent food around the table, and each person filled up his or her plate with a bit of everything. And as they began eating, the topic of conversation was of no interest to Annie whatsoever. It seemed no one could find anything more interesting to talk about other than the barn. Even Margaret joined in on the conversation, including her memory of the horrific storm that brought the barn crumbling down.

Annie was incredibly bored by all of it. She had heard it plenty of times before and was simply not interested in hearing it again. Absently, she made a trail through her potatoes with her fork, then took a chunk of the roast beef and began chewing. And as she looked up hoping to steal a glance in Will's direction, she was astonished to discover his eyes looking right back at her. They seemed to be twinkling at her.

Flustered, she quickly looked at her plate again and concentrated on her supper. She felt her cheeks growing red, and she couldn't bear for Will to see this. Annie was certain now that she was smitten with him, and it gave her a delicious tingle that ran up and down her body.

Apparently, she had been deep in thought because the next thing she knew, her mother set a slice of homemade apple pie in front of her.

Margaret's elbow poked her arm. "What is the matter with you? You have a goofy look on your face," she whispered.

"Huh?" Annie felt as though someone had splashed ice water in her face. "Oh, uh, it's nothing." Her feeble excuse pacified her friend, and Annie stuffed a huge forkful of pie in her mouth.

The meal ended a few minutes later, and the two men went outside to resume their work while the women cleared the table. Mama and Beth chattered nonstop, but Annie stayed silent. She began to realize her feelings for Will to the full extent. She had had crushes on boys before, but something about Will was different. She wasn't quite sure what to make of it.

CHAPTER 5

The weekend seemed to go by way too fast. Annie wanted to do so many things in those two short days. But now, it was Monday, and Annie sat in the tiny cramped schoolroom, sharing a seat with Danny Watkins and Marie Anderson. Miss Muldoon stood straight and tall at the front of the room beside her desk. She had just assigned a lengthy reading assignment to the older students in history. Annie jotted down the page numbers they would be tested on the next afternoon. Most of the students began their reading in hopes of having less to do at home. Annie tried, but she couldn't concentrate on anything but Will at the moment. Every time she bent her head to look at the pages of the book in front of her, his face popped into her mind. She tried vehemently to shake the thoughts from her head. She knew she had to receive high grades throughout her years in school if she wanted to become a veterinarian someday. It was her dream since she was knee high to her pa, helping him with the horses and cattle and feeding the dogs and cats that frequented the Allister farm over the years. She loved animals, and her eyes teared up every time she encountered a sick or wounded animal. Thus, she had decided long ago that even though most women around these parts didn't work outside of the home, she would be an exception. She would be the first female veterinarian the town of Gregory had seen.

Only an hour remained of school for the day, and Annie read what she could of the history lesson. And in no time at all, Miss Muldoon excused the students for the day. Annie was glad it was over because she had a special favor to do for Margaret. Today was the day she was going to nudge Carl into asking Margaret to the Fall Social.

Annie gathered up her books and lunch pail. She walked out of the school and met Margaret at the bottom of the steps. They began walking together when a familiar voice called out from behind them, "Hey, Annie! Margaret! Wait up!" It was Carl and his younger brother Andy. They sometimes all walked home together as a group since the Davis' lived near the Allisters'.

Margaret and Annie turned around and waited for the boys to catch up to them. "Why hello, boys. You are just in time," Annie said in Carl's direction.

Andy instantly grew suspicious. "For what?" he asked nervously. His freckled face held a look of concern.

Annie laughed. "Don't worry, I wasn't talking to you," she assured him and patted him on the back. Andy let out a huge sigh of relief.

But now, Carl looked nervous. "What is it, Annie?" he asked, curious.

Margaret looked uneasy and remained silent. Annie knew she was going to have to do all the talking. "Well," she said with some hesitation. She wanted only to help Margaret start a conversation with this boy, not do the entire deed herself. But since it appeared to be turning out that way, she continued boldly, "Do you have a date for the dance Saturday night?" *Nothing like blurting it out*, she thought, pleased with the courage she had exhibited.

The moment the question rolled off Annie's tongue, she regretted it. The tips of Carl's ears turned a dark shade of crimson. He looked at Annie unbelievingly. "Why, Annie, I figgered you'd have one by now."

Annie's jaw dropped. She shot Margaret a nasty look. Why didn't she speak up? If things continued the way they were, Annie would end up with Margaret's date. "Oh, I do have a date already, Carl, but you see, Margaret doesn't." Annie pointed her thumb in her friend's direction.

Carl stood for a long moment, not saying anything. He appeared confused, and even though several girls thought Carl was handsome, he wasn't considered very bright.

After what seemed an eternity, Carl's face lit up as though he had finally figured out what Annie was trying to say. "Oh." He began stammering nervously, "I-I don't have a d-date either. I was goin' to stay home that evening, but I would be happy to be your escort, Margaret."

The foursome reached The Hill at that moment, and Annie was relieved. "Thank you, boys, for keeping us company on our way home."

"Bye," the boys said in unison.

As soon as the boys were out of earshot, Annie turned to Margaret and gave her a stern punch on the arm. "Ow," Margaret shouted, rubbing the sore spot. "What was that for?"

"It was for nothing because that is exactly what you did."

Margaret's voice acquired a nasally whine to it. "What exactly did you want me to do?"

Annie was once again annoyed. Could Margaret really be so blind? "Well, for starters, you could have joined in on our conversation with the guys back there. You know, I almost ended up with Carl as my date instead of you."

Margaret's eyes went cold as she squinted evilly at her dearest friend. "Well, just go right ahead. I was going to stay home that evening anyway and work on my knitting."

Annie shook her head sternly. "Oh no, you're not. That dance is going to be way too much fun for you to hide out at home. Besides," Annie pointed out, "after all I just did to get Carl to ask you to go with him, I think you owe it to me to go."

Margaret looked thoughtful, as though she was thinking about it, then bombarded Annie with questions. "How are the both of us going to have fun when you don't even have a date yet? And just when do you plan to ask Will?"

Annie answered with overwhelming confidence. "I plan to do just that the moment I get home."

Margaret planted her hands firmly on her hips. "I don't know if I believe you."

"Just watch me," Annie challenged.

"Oh, I intend to. Let's go."

CHAPTER 6

The sun was strong as the girls reached their destination. Will was there, just as Annie had hoped. And he looked as though he could use a break.

Margaret went in the house to help Mama with the supper, and Annie headed straight for the barn to rush through her share of the chores. When she finished, she ran to the house and closely examined herself in the mirror. She didn't want to look like she had taken great pains to brush her hair, yet at the same time, she knew she looked a sight from doing her chores. She decided to comb her hair anyway. *After all*, she reasoned with herself, *I am about to ask a man I hardly know to be my date Saturday night.* The last thing she wanted to do was scare him off.

But as she took one final look at herself in her handheld mirror, a sudden attack of the jitters flowed through her entire body, giving her goose bumps. She began to doubt herself. Did she really have the courage to ask Will out? What if he said no?

For a moment, she wanted to change her mind, but then she remembered how handsome he was, and her confidence suddenly returned.

She took a deep breath and smoothed down the front of her skirt. Margaret handed her two glasses of cold lemonade. As she headed for the door, her friend whispered, "Good luck." And as Annie approached the barn, her feet felt like lead, making it even harder for her to continue.

Her heart beating wildly in her chest, Annie crept over to the north side of the barn where Will was busy hammering nails. She noticed Pa was nowhere in sight, and she knew he must've gone into town for supplies. She breathed a great sigh of relief, knowing that without Pa around, it would be that much easier to talk to Will.

Annie approached him cautiously, and he looked up from his work when he saw her. "Well, hello, Annie," he said as though he was happy to see her.

Hesitating for a second, she almost chickened out but knew this was her chance. "Thirsty?" her voice croaked. She held a glass of lemonade up in the air, the condensation making her hand cold and wet.

A huge smile spread across his face. He climbed down from the roof and accepted the drink from her. "You read my mind," he said, guzzling the refreshing drink. "Thank you. I was gettin' mighty thirsty up there."

Annie kept her composure, which was difficult standing so close to him and knowing she had done something pleasing for him. "Well, it certainly looked like you needed the break."

"I shore did."

Talking to Will was harder than Annie thought it would be, and she took a long sip of her lemonade. Only a few seconds into their conversation, and they were already at a loss for words. She looked around awkwardly, then shouted out, "The tree!"

Will was taken aback, not quite sure why Annie had shouted, but she pointed at it and said more calmly, "We could sit under that big elm tree to drink our lemonade. The shade will be cooler."

"Sounds good to me," Will agreed.

They went to the elm tree and sat down beside it. It felt good to be out of the scorching sun. Annie didn't know how Will and her pa could stand the heat for as long as they did. Annie took another nervous sip of her lemonade, barely looking at Will. She was afraid he could read her mind and know what she was thinking.

She figured she had better say something before Will became bored and went back to his work. But fortunately for her, he beat her to it. "It's a warm one today," he observed, squinting up at the relentless sun.

Annie nodded.

Will hesitated once again before plunging back into conversation. "So, Annie, tell me about yourself. I mean, your pa talks about you and your ma and your sister constantly." He paused a moment to wipe off the sweat that ran down his cheek. "But he doesn't exactly mention the important things."

Annie was curious about that comment. "What does he tell you?"

Will chuckled and did not hesitate to answer. "He says you're persistent, and I believe he even used the word stubborn once or twice."

Annie wasn't at all surprised. Her father knew everything there was to know about his daughters, and then some. He probably even knew more about them than they knew about themselves. She cocked her head to one side. "Well, what else would you like to know about me?" She would tell him anything. And she wanted to know everything about him. She longed for that intimacy with him.

Will shrugged his broad shoulders. "Whatever you want to tell me. Your hopes, your dreams, your ambitions. Your friends, school, anything. I'm new here and could use a few friends. And I can't think of a better friend to start with than you."

After that remark penetrated her ears, Annie felt bravery envelope her and knew she would be able to ask him to the dance. "Okay," Annie began. She took a deep breath before her long string of sentences. "Well, as you have probably guessed, Margaret is my best friend and has been since we were old enough to walk. You see, our fathers grew up around here and are close friends. So are our mothers, I guess. Anyway, I do well in school, but I have no choice. I have to do well because I would like to go to veterinarian school someday."

"Really?" Will sounded impressed by that.

Annie paused a moment, not knowing what else he wanted to know. "Anything else?" she asked, then blushed at the thought of offering information about herself. Even though she wanted that closeness with him, she still wasn't quite comfortable doing that, and she told him so.

He looked genuinely surprised. "Well, you could've fooled me. You did just fine," he reassured her.

"I hope so," she said, suddenly feeling shy again. "I don't have much confidence in myself." Nervously, she wiped some blades of grass from her long gingham skirt.

"I don't see why not. As far as I can tell, you are a beautiful and smart young woman, so don't sell yourself short."

"Why, thank you, Will." She was grateful for the compliment, but she decided it was time to change the subject. "Your turn."

He flashed her an odd expression. "For what?"

"To tell me about yourself."

"Oh," he said, as though returning from outer space. "Well, I'm afraid my story isn't such a happy one. You see, my folks and I and my big sister lived out west ever since I can remember. I was too young to remember any of that, and from what I'm told, my pa got word that my grandmother had passed on. Him and Ma and my sis packed up to make the trip to say their proper good-byes. I was too young to go with, so I stayed behind with my older brother, John. You remember him?"

Annie nodded, fascinated so far by the story.

Will continued, "Well, one day, only a few days later, John sat me down and told me about the train wreck." His eyes looked empty then with no memories of his family. "I've been living with John and his family ever since."

Annie was silent. She hadn't expected to hear a sad story like that. She had always assumed his family was living somewhere nearby. She touched his hand lightly. "I'm very sorry," she whispered.

But it had been a long time ago, and Will's voice sounded strong and reassuring. "It's all right. I'm all right. It was a long time ago, and I've moved on."

The two of them sat in silence for a long while until Will changed the subject. He caught Annie off guard when he began again abruptly. "I hear there's a big shindig in town on Saturday night."

Annie couldn't believe her luck. He brought up the social, and now she wouldn't have to. *Maybe I ought to check my pocket to see if there is a four-leaf clover in it*, she thought. "Uh-huh," she answered.

"John and his wife Alice have been going out of their minds looking for someone to watch the boys that evening. They brought up your name, but I told them you probably had a date."

The time had come for Annie to make her bold move. She took a deep breath. "Actually, I don't have a date yet," she confessed bravely.

He turned his head to look at her. "Really? I figgered a pretty young woman like you would've been snatched up right away."

There was that twinkle in his eyes again. "I would certainly like to go," she hinted.

Will cocked his head to one side. "I guess if you would like to accompany me, neither one of us would have to worry about finding a date," he offered with a faint eagerness in his voice.

Annie could not believe what she had heard. Had he done the asking for her? She could hardly contain herself, but she knew she had to because she didn't want Will catching on to her true feelings.

But the minute he noticed her beet red face, he apologized. "I'm sorry, Annie. I surely didn't mean to offend you with such an idea."

Annie was still in a numb state but snapped right out of it the minute she heard his remark. He had taken her reaction the wrong way. "No," she yelled at him. Then, she lowered her voice and said more calmly, "No, you didn't embarrass me. And it wasn't a bad idea at all. In fact, I would love to be your date at the social on Saturday night."

Annie could almost see her words soaking into his brain, because a few seconds later, a huge grin spread across the entire length of his face. "Then you accept?" He sounded as though he hadn't heard her right.

Annie nodded excitedly, and Will continued to grin. "I guess it's a date then." He sounded relieved.

Just then, Pa's wagon came rattling over The Hill. Will and Annie stood up. "The boss is back, so I best get back to work," Will said and handed his empty glass to Annie.

"Okay. I'll see you around, Will." After standing up, she wiped another cluster of grass from her skirt. Her legs were trembling with excitement. She desperately wanted to jump up and down and squeal delightedly over her monumental victory, but she remained calm and knew she had to tell Margaret immediately.

Margaret sat at the kitchen table having a nice talk with Mama when Annie burst in the door, grabbed hold of Margaret's arm, and rudely yanked her away from the table to the privacy of her bedroom. She knew her friend would be thrilled for her, and she was right. The two girls hugged and breathlessly discussed their thoughts on the upcoming event. "I'm so happy right now," she practically shouted in Margaret's face. Her wide smile soon turned to anguish. "Oh, I'm scared too." She paced back and forth on her bedroom floor. The one loose floorboard creaked rhythmically each time she stepped on it.

Margaret couldn't help but smile in reaction to Annie's bubbly mood. "I know you are," she replied understandingly. "But don't forget, I will be there that night, too, and we will have the best time. I promise." She smiled at her best friend and squeezed her hand lovingly.

Annie was silent throughout supper that evening. She still couldn't believe that Will had asked her to the social instead of the other way around. And to think she had been so worried about doing it herself. Absently, she rolled her peas around on her plate instead of eating them. She knew she would have to mention her date to her folks soon, but she was afraid of what they might say about her being too young for a date. It was best to tell them right away and be done with it.

Margaret had stayed for supper but left shortly afterward, and Annie tackled her difficult arithmetic homework. Then, she knew the time had come. She wrapped her shawl around her shoulders and stepped out into the chilly evening air. As she had suspected, Pa sat out by the barn smoking his pipe. He did this every night because Mama made it perfectly clear there would be no pipe smoking in her house. Mama had put her knitting away a few minutes earlier and went out to join her husband outside. Beth was still doing her schoolwork at the table.

Annie trembled as she neared her parents, although she wasn't sure why. Her folks liked Will. She hoped they would be happy for her.

"Schoolwork all done?" Pa enquired.

"Yes, sir," Annie answered.

Her mother was quick to step in. She wrapped her shawl tighter around her plump body. "It's getting late, young lady. Shouldn't you be getting off to bed?"

"Oh, I will, Mama. It's just that I need to speak with you and Pa first." Her words came out sounding more like a frog croaking than a young woman speaking.

Immediately, Mrs. Allister's face went pale. "What's wrong?" she demanded.

Annie was quick to assure her. "Nothing's wrong, Mama." She hadn't meant to startle her mother, although that wasn't hard to do. "But I would like to talk with you and Pa about something."

"All right, dear," her mother replied. Both of her parents stood beside each other and waited for her to begin.

Annie clasped her hands in front of her and looked down at her feet as she always did when she was nervous. "I thought I ought to mention something to you. You see, I got to talking to Will this afternoon, and we ended up talking about the Social. He asked me to go with him." She rocked back and forth on her heels, waiting for their disapproval. Instead, her parents looked at each other questioningly, then at Annie.

"Is that it?" her mother asked with a hint of a smirk playing on her lips.

"Yes."

Mrs. Allister threw her arms around Annie and squeezed her lovingly. "Annie, that's wonderful news. You'll have so much fun. I just know it!"

Pa's hug came next. "Great news, precious. Why were you so worried about telling us this?"

Annie had been put on the spot. She herself wasn't quite sure. "Uh, I, well, I guess I don't know exactly. Maybe it's because he is so much older than me," she guessed. But she also knew it was because she was embarrassed. This would be her very first date.

But Mama just brushed it off. "Well, that is just nonsense. It's not like the two of you are getting hitched. You're just going to a dance together as friends to become better acquainted."

"You mean you're not upset?" Annie asked, already feeling relieved.

Pa looked surprised. "Now, why would we be upset? You couldn't have picked a finer gentleman to go with. Will is an exceptional young man, and I'm happy for you." Pa reached over and tousled her hair just like he used to do when she was younger, but this time, she didn't mind. He flashed a smile at his wife and went inside the house.

Annie glanced at her mother whose face beamed with pride. "Come on, dear." She squeezed Annie's hand and led her back to the house. "Tomorrow we'll pick out something special for you to wear." She looked thoughtful for a moment, then expressed her thoughts. "Maybe that new dress I made you for your birthday. And your Sunday hair clips will do nicely."

Annie only smiled and didn't say a word. She was somewhat frightened. This would be her first date, and she thought her parents should have tried to protect her somehow. After all, what if Will wanted to kiss her? The thought made Annie feel both terrified and excited. She wanted to kiss Will more than anything, but she had never kissed a boy before and feared she might do it wrong. *But*, she thought, shrugging, *if Pa and Mama aren't worried, then neither should I be.*

And as Annie nodded off to sleep that night, she dreamed of nothing but Will and his strong, full lips caressing her own.

CHAPTER 7

Saturday arrived, and it turned out to be one of the longest days of Annie's life. She woke up feeling nauseated and nervous. Would she impress Will enough so he would ask her out again? She threw on an everyday dress and went to the kitchen, figuring she would find out soon enough.

As she expected, the house buzzed with the usual morning activities. It felt cold in the little kitchen. September mornings were always quite chilly, prompting Pa to throw some logs onto the fire. They rushed through breakfast so everyone could finish their daily chores more quickly and have more time to dress for their big evening.

Every member of the Allister family was going to the Social, and each had their own chores to be responsible for that day. Annie knew she and Mama had the best jobs of them all. After taking the eggs into town to the mercantile, they rushed home and spent the afternoon hemming dresses and picking out jewelry from Mama's trunk of treasures.

Annie always enjoyed these times when she and her mother spent time together, just the two of them. She hated to see these special times come to an end.

But this one did when Mama exclaimed, "Goodness. It's almost time for supper. I think Beth has it done. I can smell it."

Annie laid the beautiful jewelry back in Mama's antique trunk, which was lined with delicate tissue paper. She and Beth had been allowed to choose one piece each to wear tonight. She knew Beth would choose the broach that Mama had received from her mother when she was a young girl, which made Annie's choice simple. She reached in and slowly pulled out the delicate string of pearls her mother had worn on her wedding day. It was a stunning piece, the dull glimmer a reminder of how beautiful her mother must have looked that day. Annie felt proud every time she wore it around her neck. Mama stood up and started for the kitchen, and Annie shot her mother an anxious look. "Mama?" she asked in a hoarse voice.

Her mother whirled around to face her. "Yes, dear?"

"Is everything … okay … for tonight?" Annie was unable to find the right words, but her mother understood what she was asking.

"Annie, you have nothing to worry about. Everything will go just fine." She walked back over to her daughter and gently embraced her. "You will have such a good time tonight you won't even think about being nervous." Annie still looked unsure, and her mother flashed her a huge reassuring smile. "Well, you'll see. And as we've said before, Will is a wonderful young man. We're delighted you two are going together. Okay?"

Annie nodded dumbly, and the two women left the room together, heading for the kitchen table and the delicious meal Beth had prepared.

As Annie sat at the table enjoying the mouth-watering roast beef, she began to feel better. Mama's speeches always seemed to lift her spirits. *And besides*, she thought smugly, taking a second slab of the roast, *going out on a date with Will is exactly what I've wanted since the day I first saw him. There is no reason to be glum.*

Supper passed by unusually quickly, and once the dishes had been washed, everyone put their best clothes on. Annie and Beth looked incredibly stunning as they went into their mother's room to fetch the jewelry their mother promised they could borrow. The girls and their ma put on their jewels, and everyone piled into Pa's wagon for the bumpy ride into town.

As they entered the little town, Annie felt the butterflies in her stomach and sensed the excitement in the air. Everywhere she looked, there were people bustling about in their Sunday best. A group of young, giggling girls entered the restaurant where the dance was to be held.

Pa's wagon came to a stop beside the others on the dirt road, and he helped his wife and daughters down, exclaiming, "Your escorts will be proud!"

Just then, Andy Davis, Beth's date for the evening, strolled up to her. "Hello, Beth," his adolescent voice cracked. "You look pretty." The tips of his ears were bright pink. Annie rolled her eyes. That sounded so rehearsed. Beth and Andy walked off together, as did Mama and Pa, but not before telling her to have a great time.

Annie scanned the crowd of people entering the restaurant in hopes of catching sight of Will, but no such luck. She heaved a great sigh, then trudged up to the steps and entered the restaurant.

Her eyes swept the room, and she was amazed at what she saw. Mrs. Wilkins, the manager, did an excellent job with the decorating. All the tables and chairs had been completely removed from the dining area, which would serve as the dance floor. Leaves that were already turning golden had been scattered all across the floor. And there were corn husks hung evenly on the walls between the windows. But Annie's favorite part of all was a scarecrow that had been brought in from someone's corn field and propped up by the door and dressed in a tuxedo. Mrs. Wilkins had achieved the look of autumn, and the place looked absolutely enchanting.

With wide eyes, Annie watched for Will to come walking in. A horrifying thought occurred to her. Maybe he decided not to show up. She could instantly feel the tips of her ears grow red with fury. He had better not pull a stunt like that on her.

But just then, as though reading her mind, he appeared in the doorway as if by magic.

For a moment, he took her breath away. She was stunned at how much more handsome he was tonight. His short brown hair was slicked back, and he was clean-shaven. He wore a dark blue shirt with a matching tie. Annie had only seen him in his work clothes before, and the way he looked tonight was a nice improvement.

Annie felt awkward and wasn't quite sure what to do. She stared at him for a long moment. The nervous feeling had returned. It was all she could do to keep from running out of there as fast as she could.

But Will had noticed her. He wore a wide grin on his face, and he waved to her as he walked toward her. "Evenin', Annie," he greeted her as every young lady present stared enviously in her direction.

"Hello," she said and felt silly that her voice trembled so. She knew she must relax to have a good time this evening. And before any other words were exchanged, Will clasped Annie's hand in his and led her out on to the dance floor where they danced gracefully three waltzes in a row.

Except for a few breaks here and there, they danced together the entire night. Annie's cheeks were sore from all the smiling and laughing she had done. She had taken her mother's advice and loosened up, glad that she had.

As more and more couples sat down for rests, Will decided to treat Annie to some of the finest cookies in town, which had been made by his sister-in-law. They walked over to the refreshment table hand in hand, and Annie spotted Carl and Margaret. She waved excitedly to them.

The couple joined Will and Annie, and Margaret threw her arms around Annie in an aggressive embrace. "What on earth was that for?" she asked her friend as she tried to catch her breath from having it squeezed out of her.

Margaret's face was glowing. "Oh, Annie," she exclaimed, "I am having such a wonderful time tonight." She lowered her voice and pointed her thumb in Carl's direction. "He is wonderful."

"I am so happy I was able to help you. Whatever makes you happy makes me happy too." She glanced over at her own date and realized she should get back to him. "I'll talk to you later." She was purely overjoyed for her friend and was glad to be able to bring her and Carl together.

Will and Annie danced one last dance together and realized the event was beginning to die down. Annie was tired anyway and ready to find her folks in the crowd, but Will had other ideas. "I could drive you home. I-If you'd like me to," he offered cautiously.

"Would you?" Annie asked, not sure she had heard him right.

He chuckled. "Well, sure I will. Why don't you go on and tell your folks you're leavin'?"

"I looked around for them and don't see them. I think they went home already."

Will shrugged. "Well, then, I best get you home too." He held out his hand, and Annie took it. Shivers ran up her spine as their hands made contact, and Annie climbed onto the wagon with Will's help. He climbed up after her and began driving in the direction of her home.

By then, it was well past dark, but Annie still managed to sneak a quick glance or two at Will's face. She had become enamored by his stunning good looks.

Will drove on. It was a rough road, and Annie felt like a paddle ball on the hard wagon seat. The silence was uncomfortable, and Annie was relieved when Will finally said something. "What did you think of those sugar cookies?" he asked.

That seemed to be an odd question, but she knew he was trying to make conversation. "Oh, they were delicious," she replied. She turned to look at him. "Why do you ask?"

"My brother's wife, Alice, made them."

"Well, you can tell her they didn't last half the night. I think they were gone before sundown."

Will's hearty laugh rang out in the darkness. "There's no cook quite like her."

Annie wagged her finger at him. "Oh, now wait a minute. You have tasted my mama's cooking. Or have you forgotten? Now she truly is the finest cook around."

Will nodded. "I can't argue with you there. Maybe she will invite me to supper again real soon. You know, since I work with your pa and all."

Annie grinned. "I'm sure she will. Mama loves to entertain guests." And that was when Will drove up to the door of her house.

It was a chilly evening, and Annie's teeth chattered, but she didn't budge from her seat. She knew they needed to say good night first.

"I guess this is good night," Will said somberly.

"I guess so." Neither one of them budged, and Annie was shivering by this time. "I really want to thank you for a lovely evening," she said to Will.

"Oh, I enjoyed it every bit as much as you did. I'll see you tomorrow in church. Here, take my hand."

Annie took hold of his hand while she climbed down from the wagon. "Good night, Will. See you tomorrow."

They waved to each other as Will drove away and was swallowed up by the dark night. And although she was freezing in the frosty autumn air, she stood in the darkness watching him as he headed for home.

She went in the house, and her family was already sitting at the table drinking hot tea and waiting for her. "Did you have fun, dear?" Her mother asked with a hint of eagerness in her meek voice. She poured a steaming mug of tea for her daughter.

"Oh, Mama!" Annie was breathless from the brisk air outside. "I had the most wonderful time. And Will is one of the sweetest men I have ever met." She rolled her eyes. "Honestly, I don't know what I was so nervous about." She stopped short. Had she really described her date as sweet in front of her parents? She was horrified, and her face flushed. What on earth would they think?

But she needn't have worried. They just beamed proudly at her. "I knew you would have a good time," her mother said matter-of-factly.

And Pa chimed in, "I knew the moment I met him that Will was a fine fellow."

Annie had to admit her folks always did know best. That was one of the many reasons she loved and respected them so much.

She finished up the last of her tea and stood up from her chair. "Boy," she yawned, "I sure am tuckered. I think I'm going to go to bed." She said good night to her mother and father and kissed and hugged each of them.

She went straight to her snug bed and pulled Mama's handmade quilt up to her chin. She had figured on falling right to sleep, but her mind kept drifting back to her date. How handsome Will had been! And so very charming. And it was at that precise moment that Annie knew Will was the man she would someday marry.

CHAPTER 8

The next morning was sunny, although an autumn chill hung heavily in the air. It was a great relief to the entire Allister family to arrive at the church. "It's so chilly this morning," Beth said with a shudder, stuffing her hands in the pockets of her coat.

Everyone scurried into the toasty little church and found their usual pew. Annie rubbed her hands together to warm them up and noticed just about everyone else was doing the same. It was cold days like this that made everyone in Gregory appreciate the rattling coal stove in the back of the room despite how distracting it was.

She looked around anxiously to catch sight of Will, but she didn't see him. Disappointed, she turned to face forward and opened her Bible, although she had trouble concentrating on it. Annie certainly hoped Will was a God-fearing person, or her family might not approve of him after all.

Reverend Johnston interrupted her thoughts when he walked down the narrow aisle and took his place before the congregation. He was a thin, frail man with gray hair and tiny spectacles. When they were younger, Annie and Beth thought he was a funny-looking little man and had to try very hard not to burst into giggles at the sight of him. They didn't dare laugh because Pa would have given them a licking when they returned home. But despite his meek appearance, Reverend Johnston was a bold, intelligent man with a booming voice, and his messages touched every single person fortunate enough to hear them. Today's sermon was no exception. Today, he spoke about what it meant to love God and others equally.

Mrs. Allister always stressed to her daughters the importance of paying attention in church, but today, Annie only picked up bits and pieces of the service. She just couldn't keep her mind off of Will. Why hadn't he come this morning? When they parted yesterday, he said he would see her in church. Why would he say that if he wasn't going to show up?

It was a great relief to Annie when they finished singing the closing hymn. She always enjoyed the Sunday sermons, but today, she couldn't concentrate. Reverend Johnston made his closing remarks. After he finished, everyone stood up and greeted one another. And as Annie turned to go, she stopped short.

There he was, only two rows behind her. *That sneak*, she thought. *He must've slipped quietly in right after I stopped watching for him.* At first, Annie panicked. She didn't know if she should talk to him or pretend she hadn't seen him.

But there was no denying they had seen each other, and again, Annie felt her cheeks turning red.

The Allister family walked toward the door, and as they passed Will, Annie glanced cautiously at Will, who was already looking at her. He nodded at her, and she flashed him a sweet smile.

And that was it. That was all she would see of him for that day.

Or so she thought.

* * *

It was a tradition in the Allister house to have Mama's homemade chicken soup on Sundays after church. The family never grew tired of this hearty meal. Annie remembered Pa once made a joke about the cows giving better milk just from the smell of the soup. Of course, she believed it then, but not anymore. She was old enough to know better now.

The family finished their delicious, peaceful meal, and then the womenfolk cleared off the table and washed the dishes. As they worked, they heard Pup bark in a friendly tone. Pa went over to the window and took a look outside. "Well," he exclaimed, "looks like we've got us some company." This was rare on a Sunday, unless it was Reverend Johnston, and the girls exchanged anxious looks with each other. They couldn't wait to see who had arrived.

But the second Annie glanced out the window, she immediately felt the butterflies fluttering about inside of her. It was him. Will had come to see her! She wanted so desperately to see him, but not with her family around. It was all she could do to fly out the door before the rest of her family reached him. But they were already at his side by the time Annie stepped outside. Pa greeted Will with a hearty slap on the back.

"Afternoon," Will said, tipping his hat.

"Hi, Will," Beth said, swaying back and forth and fluttering her eyelids. Annie rolled her eyes. Beth's crush on Will was so obvious.

"We just ate," Mama chimed in. "I'm sorry you missed it."

"Aw, it's alright. Alice fed me good at home," Will assured Mama before turning to Annie and tipping his hat at her. "Uh, hi, Annie."

"Hi, Will." They both looked down at the ground. An uncomfortable silence hung in the air.

Pa's voice shattered the awkward moment. "So, what brings you out this way, son? Seems to me I gave you Sundays off."

Will chuckled. "Indeed you did, sir. Actually, I was wonderin' if you'd want to go fishin' with me. You know, show me where all the best places are and all."

Pa's face brightened. "I sure would. Just give me a minute to fetch my pole." He headed for the barn where he kept it and returned a moment later.

Once again, Will tipped his hat to the ladies. "I'll see all of you tomorrow," he said as he and Pa walked down the path leading to the fishing hole.

The men reached the barn before Mama spoke. "Beth, if you still want to learn to knit, I can show you now. I'm about to start," she offered. She put her arm around Beth's shoulders, and the two of them walked back into the house together.

Annie remained rooted to the ground, too upset to move. She could not believe after the enchanting evening they had spent together the night before that Will had barely spoken two words to her just now.

She walked back to the house as if there was lead in her shoes. And for the remainder of the day, she sat in her room, trying desperately to study for tomorrow's arithmetic exam. It was no use. Her mind was swamped with thoughts of Will. Why had he ignored her in such a way? Had she done something last night to offend him?

CHAPTER 9

The exam went surprisingly well the next morning. Annie received the second-highest mark of all the students. The only one with a perfect score was Mary Monroe, the smartest girl in the entire school. Annie couldn't help but wonder what marks she would have gotten had she been able to concentrate on her studying yesterday.

On the way home from school that afternoon, Annie told Margaret all about yesterday's happenings.

"I thought your date went well." Margaret sounded confused.

"So did I," Annie said and shook her head. "I just don't understand what I did wrong."

Suddenly, Margaret's face lit up mischievously. She let out an evil cackle. "Silly girl. You didn't do anything wrong."

"I didn't?"

"No, of course not. You did everything you should have."

"What do you mean?" Annie demanded.

The two girls had reached The Hill. Margaret twirled Annie around to face her. "Don't you see?"

"No, I don't," Annie cried impatiently.

Margaret rolled her eyes. "I'd say Will likes you more than you think."

Annie's mouth fell open as she began to realize what her friend was trying to explain to her. She found it hard to speak. "But, that can't--it just can't be. I mean, if he likes me so much, wouldn't he be nicer to me than he was earlier?"

"Oh, Annie," Margaret sounded irritated. "I always thought you knew more about this kind of thing than I did." She hesitated as Annie remained clueless. "I guess I was wrong." Annie continued to say nothing, and Margaret sighed heavily.

Margaret explained herself to Annie as though Annie were a young child. "Will is a young man, and young men are difficult to understand. Sometimes they will treat you badly so you won't know how they really feel. It's true. A similar thing happened to my cousin, who eventually ended up marrying the man."

Margaret glanced in the direction of her home. "Look, Annie, I best be going. Just think about what I said. I know I am right about this one." She squeezed Annie's hand, said good-bye, and ran home.

Annie walked home as well. She was too stunned by what her friend had said to care if she was late for chores. Was Will really interested in her? She hoped so with all her might.

Just then, an incredible thought came to her. If Margaret was right and Will really was interested in her, then maybe the two of them would become an item. The thought of it gave her the chills.

Annie set her books and lunch pail in the shade beside the barn and cleaned out the stalls. She knew perfectly well Will was up on the roof hammering nails. It was so loud she couldn't miss it.

Annie thought about how handsome he was. She was excited because of what Margaret had said, yet at the same time, she was upset at how he had acted toward her, and she was going to do her best to avoid him because of it.

The next thing she knew, she heard a tremendous thump, followed by groaning.

Annie knew exactly what had happened. She threw the rake on the ground and ran outside. She was right. Will was sprawled out on the parched, dusty ground.

"Will!" Annie screamed frantically. She rushed over to him and laid his head gently in her lap. "What happened, Will?" Annie's voice trembled.

"I just lost my balance," he explained in a voice much calmer than her own.

Annie patted Will's arm. "Well, I can see that." She raised an eyebrow at him. "Are you okay?"

"Yeah. Yeah, I think so."

Annie breathed a sigh of relief. "Thank goodness."

Will groaned and struggled to sit up. "I think my arm is broken, though." He looked helplessly at it.

"I'll have Pa drive you into town to see the doc. Wait here." Annie started to stand up, but Will gripped her arm firmly.

"Just wait." Will looked unsure of himself, almost nervous. "I-I wanted to talk to you about something. Something important."

"What is it?" Annie asked, although judging from his uneasiness, she wasn't at all sure she wanted to hear what he had to say.

Will eyed the ground and fiddled with a fallen tree branch.

Annie sensed he was preoccupied with something, so she asked again, more urgently this time, "What was it that you wanted to talk to me about?"

It took him a long time, but finally he opened up. "I just wanted you to know that I had a good time. You know, on Saturday night. It was a really nice time."

Annie wanted to blurt out, "That's it?" But she admired his courage and said instead, "I'm glad. I enjoyed myself as well."

Will flashed her a grateful smile. "That's good." He looked her straight in the eye. Once again, he wore that uncomfortable expression. "Listen, Annie," Will's voice suddenly sounded brave, "I've been having these feelings."

Annie nodded, but she just could not understand what he was trying to say. "What kind of feelings?"

Will seemed to grow more uncomfortable every minute. He chewed his fingernails as tiny beads of perspiration glistened on his forehead. "Well, you know, serious feelings." He looked up at her timidly. "For you."

It took a minute to sink in, but when it did, Annie was completely shocked. Had she heard him correctly? If she had, it meant Margaret was right about Will's strange behavior. Excitement welled up inside of her along with a fear that made her tremble.

Will continued. He had come this far. It was too late to stop now. "We have become good friends, but I want more than that with you. I want you to be my girl."

Annie felt her lips quiver. She had to think fast. This was what she wanted, and she could not mess it up. "I'd like that" was all she said, and she gently touched his hand.

Will's eyes had been nervously boring a hole in his boots, but upon hearing that, his eyes lit up, and relief washed over his face.

The next moment was pure magic for Annie. She turned to Will to smile at him, but instead, their lips locked in a tender, beautiful kiss. They embraced afterward, and to Annie, it seemed to be over much too quickly.

"Now, how about that ride to the doc's office?" Will asked her, abruptly changing the subject.

"Of course," Annie said, helping Will up. She had completely forgotten about his fall. "Pa's inside with Mama right now." And the two walked to the tiny farmhouse with Annie's arms wrapped securely around Will's muscular body.

The doctor visit went quite well. Will had a sprain, which was easily fixed. "C'mon, son," Pa said to Will, slapping him on the shoulder. He had not been surprised at all by Will's injury. It was the kind of thing that happened all the time with farm work. "I'll give you a ride home." Annie and the two men crawled into Pa's wagon as Pa steered the team south of town in the direction of the Montgomery place.

"It's a terrible shame what happened," Pa said remorsefully, nodding at Will's bandaged arm. "I don't know where I'll find another worker who works quite as hard as you did."

Will shook his head. "I shoulda been more careful," he admitted shamefully.

But Pa disagreed. "Aw, don't be silly. Coulda happened to anyone. Matter of fact, it did. To me. Years and years ago while I was helpin' my own pa."

Will looked at him then, caught his sly smile and twinkling eyes, and the two men burst into a fit of laughter.

"Well, it did," Pa said, gasping for air. "So, you see, it really can happen to the best of us."

Again, the two men laughed together. When they had contained themselves, Will said, "I'll certainly try to visit whenever I can."

Pa gave Will a fatherly smile. "We'll all enjoy that."

"Yeah, Will," Annie piped up excitedly. "That would be great." She looked at him nervously, hoping he wouldn't think she was too eager, but he just smiled back at her affectionately.

Annie felt warm and happy inside, and as the two men went on talking about farming and other things Annie considered boring, an unsettling thought struck her. It had just occurred to Annie how hard it was going to be to see Will now that he wouldn't be helping Pa with the barn anymore. What would this do to their newfound romance?

For a moment, Annie was crushed. She never asked for much in life, and now when she finally did, it was being taken away.

She sadly looked up at Will, then soon forgot her woes. How silly she was acting! She could always go out to his place to visit, and he could do the same. She began to feel better.

Pa's wagon went up a steep hill and around a corner. There stood the Montgomery farm, nestled between two groves of ancient oak trees. Annie noticed at first glance that both the house and the farm were small and shabby. Shingles dangled on the roof of the house, and two of the porch steps had great gaps in them.

A tall, frail woman stood at the wash line hanging the day's wash out to dry. Annie guessed right away that she was John's wife, Alice. Annie waved politely to her, but Alice ignored her. Instead, she growled, "Where have you been, William? You're late."

Will turned red in the face. "I reckon I better explain." He said a quick good-bye to Annie and Graham Allister and promised he would come by soon for a visit.

As Pa drove off, two little boys scampered out of the barn to greet Will and ran through the clothes on the wash line, prompting a stern scolding from their mother. Pa and Annie looked at each other and laughed. Annie decided they must be a close, loving family.

CHAPTER 10

Every day, the weather grew colder and colder. November had just begun, and a carpet of red and gold leaves blanketed the Allister farm. Annie always paid extra attention to the crunching sound they made when she stepped on them on her way home from school.

Two weeks had passed since she had last seen Will. She did not know what to make of it. He had said himself that he wanted her for his girl. *Well*, she thought icily, *it will be hard to have a relationship if we are never together.*

Up until now, Annie had waited eagerly every day for a visit from Will. She thought it was the man's job to call on the lady. But she knew he was shy, and she made up her mind that she would make a trip out to his place tomorrow. She wouldn't be going to school anyway because Mama needed her to run a few errands for her.

The next morning, Annie washed the breakfast dishes and made her bed. Then, in her sweetest tone, she asked her mother, "Mama, do you mind if I take a bit longer than usual to come home from town? I thought I would stop by Will's place and see how he is getting along."

Mama smiled curiously. "That'll be fine, dear. Just be home before dinner. Oh, and pick up the mail if you remember."

A huge smile spread across Annie's face. "I will. Thank you, Mama."

"Have a nice time," Mama said. Annie bundled up and bounced happily out the door, but she stopped short the minute she stepped outside. The fierce November wind hit Annie's cheeks like a blast of ice water. She pulled her red wool scarf up to rest on the bridge of her nose. She was grateful Mama had made it for her for Christmas last year.

It almost seemed as though she would not make the three-mile walk into town. She was walking against the wind, and she had to fight it every step of the way. But she finally did reach town, and she scrambled inside the post office. Miss Graham smiled at her. She was always very friendly to Annie and everyone else in town. She was like a grandmother to all of the young people in town, and she soon acquired that nickname. Her frail hand slid a battered envelope across the desk to Annie. It was a letter with unfamiliar handwriting scrawled across the front and addressed to Mama. Annie wondered who it was from.

She slipped the letter inside her wide jacket pocket and continued in the direction of Will's place. The chilling wind seemed to be dying down now, which made it a bit easier to walk.

The town wasn't very busy this particular morning. Annie guessed it was due to the weather. Most people preferred to stay inside on days like this unless it was absolutely necessary to go out. When she heard a wagon faintly rattling down the frozen road in the distance, she stopped and turned to see who it could be.

Annie's heart skipped a beat when she realized it was Will. But someone else was with him. Annie could tell it was a woman, but with her wraps covering her from head to toe, it was impossible to see who it was. She knew it couldn't be Alice. Alice was an unhappy person and whoever was with Will was smiling and laughing. They both were. They seemed to be enjoying themselves.

But when Will's wagon finally came close enough for Annie to make out who his passenger was, her curiosity turned to jealousy. It was Margaret.

Annie waved her arms wildly in the air, hoping to catch their attention, but they didn't even look in her direction. They were too busy with each other to notice her.

The wagon sped right past her until it was a tiny speck in the distance. Annie stood rooted to the ground, her eyes following them the entire time. Jealousy pulsated throughout her body. She stared at the now empty road for several minutes before continuing walking. What had just happened? Her best friend and her beau had completely ignored her.

And to make matters worse, Annie was quite certain Margaret had seen her.

The brutal wind picked up suddenly, and the frozen air penetrated Annie's thick woolen jacket. She came to a fork in the road and was about to head in the direction of Will's place when a thought struck her. Could Will actually be in love with Margaret instead of her? Maybe he had been all along and had been faking his feelings for Annie only to get closer to Margaret.

Annie felt sick to her stomach realizing all of this. She recalled seeing Will turn his wagon in the direction of Margaret's place. Suddenly, her confusion turned to anger. Blinding anger. The nerve of that man! And Margaret. What kind of friend would do this kind of thing? She knew Annie had strong feelings for Will.

Well, she thought determinedly, *I will not go out without a fight first. I will get to the bottom of this*. And she marched out to the Wilson farm with a fire inside her that made her forget all about the nipping cold.

Annie hoped with all her might that, for some reason, she would not find Will there. But as she approached, she stopped short. Her heart sank. Sure enough, Will's wagon was parked right there for all the world to see.

She clenched her fists and took a deep breath. So much anger surged inside of her that she vowed right then and there that she never wanted to speak to either of them ever again.

Annie turned on her heels and was about to head home when the door of the house opened, and Will and Margaret stepped out. Margaret glanced at Will and shivered. Then, they both giggled and ran to the warmth of the barn.

She decided to follow them and confront them. Annie needed to find out what was going on between the two of them. Old Blue, the Wilson's family dog, who had been named for his bright blue eyes, jumped up and tried to lick her. She had always been fond of Old Blue because he and Pup were brothers abandoned by their mother. Margaret's father had found the entire litter near the river, exploring the area clumsily, not straying too far from each other. Their newborn whimpers and squeaks were too much for Mr. Wilson to handle. He scooped all five of them up and took them home where his family instantly fell in love with them. Of course, he gave Annie the first pick of the litter, but she found it difficult to choose. Her love for animals made her want to take them all home with her, but Pa had agreed to only one, and Mr. Wilson made sure the others all went to good homes. "Go away," she muttered to the familiar dog. She wasn't in the mood to be playful right now.

The minute Annie reached the barn door, she gave it an unnecessarily hard shove, causing it to bang into the wall.

Startled by the sudden loud noise, Margaret and Will looked up in surprise. Annie's voice was icy as she turned to look Will straight in the eye. "Now I know why you haven't come around lately. You are not interested in me at all, are you, Will Montgomery?" Annie's entire body shook with anger.

Will stared at her with big question marks in his deep-set blue eyes. She did not wait for him to answer. "And I don't think you ever were." She threw a menacing glance in Margaret's direction before turning on her.

"And you," she accused. "What kind of friend are you? You know how I feel about Will. How could you sneak around with him behind my back?"

Margaret began to tremble, and tears welled up in her eyes. It startled Annie to think she had upset dear Margaret in such a way, yet she could not stop herself. She unleashed all her hurt and anger on two of the people she loved the most. Turning again to Will, she exploded, "Are you calling on her now?"

"Now, you wait just one minute, Annie," Will scolded. "I don't know what you think is going on here. I have an idea, but it is pure nonsense. Now, let me explain."

Annie stood with her hands on her hips and didn't say a word. She had never seen Will angry before, and it almost scared her.

Will spoke when he was certain Annie would be quiet long enough to let him. "Okay. I gave Margaret a ride home because of the ugly weather. I was invited in for a cup of tea before going out in the cold again. Margaret wanted to show me her father's new horse, and that is how we ended up out here."

"Remember, I told you about that, Annie?" Margaret timidly piped up.

Annie wasn't sure of what to say. All the things he said sounded valid, especially the part about the horse. She knew he was fond of them. He always cared for his brother's horses in the hopes of owning one of his own one day. The angry barrier she had built up between herself and the two of them started to slowly crumble away.

Will said one more thing that further convinced Annie she had acted like a complete fool. "I was just about to stop out at your place to see you," he said softly. She saw the genuineness in his eyes as he looked at her. He stepped closer to her and gently put his hands on her waist. He kissed her rosy cheek lightly. "I love you," he whispered almost inaudibly.

Now, Annie felt even more humiliated. If a man told a woman he loved her, he couldn't possibly have his eye on someone else. Could he? She couldn't control them any longer, and the tears began rolling out of her eyes. She returned Will's embrace and held him tightly as though he was trying to get away. "I am so sorry for accusing you of all those silly things," she choked through her tears. "I don't know what I was thinking."

"I can imagine how it musta looked," Will whispered, stroking her hair.

Annie pulled away from him and looked passionately into his eyes. "I've been such a fool. Can you ever forgive me?"

"Oh, Annie, sweetheart. Annie, Annie, Annie. Of course I forgive you. I love you."

"And I love you, Will," Annie replied whole-heartedly. She stood on the tips of her toes as the two of them kissed softly.

As their lips parted, Annie looked eagerly over Will's shoulder. She wanted to apologize to Margaret for treating her so horribly, but her friend was nowhere in sight.

"Oh," Annie cried in despair. "I wanted to apologize to Margaret."

"It's likely she went inside so we could be alone," he said knowingly, his arms still enveloping Annie's waist. "I'm sure she'll understand if you wait."

"You're probably right."

"It's getting late and colder every minute," Will informed her as he looked up at the dusty gray sky. "Can I drive you home?"

Annie reached up and gave Will a quick but loving peck on the cheek. "That's a silly question. Of course you can. And who knows?" she smiled up at him. "Mama might even have some tea waiting for us."

He smiled back. "More tea? How could I refuse that?" They walked to the wagon. His strong hands gently helped her up to the seat of his buckboard before climbing up as well.

The wagon jerked forward roughly, and Annie huddled closely against Will's strong, burly body to keep warm. The temperature declined rapidly, but Annie only felt warmth radiating from Will. She enjoyed touching him, and she regretted that she could see the Allister farm right up the road.

They pulled into the yard, and Will stopped the wagon abruptly. He scurried over to Annie to help her down. She firmly grasped his hand as he all but lifted her down from her seat. They bustled inside, and Will firmly shut the door.

"Land sakes," Mama exclaimed, noticing their bright red cheeks and chattering teeth. "It's so cold out. Get yourselves over here by the fire and warm up a bit. I'll pour you some tea." She hurried about in the kitchen while Will and Annie stood by the fireplace, peeling off their coats and scarves. They smiled secretly to one another about the tea remark.

"I told you so," Annie whispered.

Mama poured the tea and came out of the kitchen, her skirt flying behind her. She set a wooden tray holding the three ceramic blue mugs on the kitchen table, which looked beautiful as usual. Mama always made sure it looked fantastic since it was one of the first things folks see when they come in the door. Today, it had a vase of artificial flowers adorning it along with her favorite figurine, a porcelain cat with sapphire eyes given to her by her aunt the day she married Pa.

Will had already chosen a seat, and Annie reached for the one nearest him and then remembered the letter. "Oh, I almost forgot," she exclaimed. She went over to the coat hook and pulled the now-crumpled envelope out of her coat pocket. "Here's the mail, Mama," she said and handed the shabby envelope to her mother.

Her mother scowled at her. She did not like it when Annie mistreated the mail like that. What if it had been something important? She pulled a hair pin from her hair and swiftly slid it under the flap of the envelope, opening it with ease. She scanned the letter. "My goodness," she exclaimed as tears welled up in her beautiful brown eyes.

At first, Annie was frightened that it might be bad news. "What is it, Mama?"

And just like that, a huge smile spread across Mama's entire face. "It's from your Aunt Frances."

Annie's face went blank, so Mama explained. "My big sister. Oh, we haven't seen her since you were five years old, Annie. It's been so long." Mama continued reading the neatly written letter to herself, numerous facial expressions spreading across her face.

Annie sipped her tea and began to fidget. "Would you read it to us, Mama?" she asked impatiently.

But Mama gave her daughter a long, thoughtful glance. "I'm afraid it isn't such good news after all." Then, she sighed. "But, you'll find out soon enough, I suppose." She cleared her throat and began. "'My dearest Graham, Lily, and family, I regret that it has taken me so long to put pen to paper, but recent circumstances have made it necessary to contact you. I will get right to the point. Not three weeks ago, we had a terrible prairie fire stretching from two miles north of our farm to ten miles south of it. It took the effort of all of Henry and our dear neighbors to fight it, but the flames outsmarted them. I'm sorry to say Henry perished in the fire that day. He was so brave during the entire ordeal. He sent Samantha and me to town to stay in the hotel while he braved the fire. And that day, when he kissed us good-bye was the last we ever saw of him. We miss him terribly but know that life must go on, and with no home, we must make a brand-new start. The beginning of December, we will arrive in your town, hoping our opportunity lies there. We may need to be put up awhile until we can find a proper home and jobs. If it is not too much trouble, I would appreciate you taking the time to make arrangements for us with the hotel in town. There is so much for us to catch up on, but we can do it when we are together again. I am anxious to see all of you once again. Until then, Frances.'"

Mama laid the letter down slowly and gently, almost as though it were porcelain and might break if she moved any faster. She looked solemnly at Will and Annie, who sat paralyzed in her chair. The news in Aunt Frances' letter was so terrible. But on the other hand, there was her cousin Samantha. It had been such a long time ago, and the memories were fuzzy but wonderful as well.

Samantha was three years older than Annie and always acted like a mother toward her. She was kind and gentle, always letting Annie play with her dolls, even letting her keep one once.

Annie was elated. "Oh, Will," she cried, "you will simply love my cousin. She is wonderful! I can't wait for you to meet her!"

Will's eyes twinkled at her. "I'm sure I will like her." He squeezed her hand affectionately as the three of them exchanged pleasantries and finished their mugs of tea.

The afternoon flew quickly by and the time came for Will to be on his way. He rose from the table. "Thank you, Mrs. Allister, for the lovely afternoon and the tea. It was good." He bundled up to battle the extreme temperatures outside.

Mama brushed off his comment. "Don't you mention it, Will. You're welcome here anytime, you know that. And please, call me Lillian."

"Okay, I will," he chuckled. He turned to Annie, who stood only inches from him, suddenly feeling shy.

"Good-bye, Annie. I'll try stopping by again tomorrow." Will kissed her lips tenderly, lightly, and with a wave of his gloved hand, he was gone.

Not even a second had passed since the door had shut, and Annie already missed him terribly. And even though he said he would try visiting tomorrow, she knew it would seem like an eternity. But she went into the kitchen to help Mama bake bread for the next day. She diligently kneaded the dough on the floured tabletop and felt an emptiness in her heart unlike anything she had ever felt before. She had begun to realize how strong her love for Will had become, and she hoped with all her heart to someday become Mrs. Montgomery.

CHAPTER 11

Over the next few weeks, Annie and Will spent as much time together in the evenings as they could. Annie had school to attend during the day and Will had to work, but they made the most of their evenings. The young couple would go for romantic rides in Will's buckboard or slow walks holding hands along the lakeside where the leaves on the willow trees danced calmly in the chilly evening air.

Only one day of school remained before Thanksgiving, and Annie could hardly wait. She found it difficult to concentrate on her schoolwork, much less copying off the blackboard the extra homework assignments the teacher wanted her pupils to work on while they were away from school.

It seemed almost an eternity, but at last Miss Muldoon said the words Annie and all the other children longed to hear. "Okay, students, you may go quietly to the cloakroom and put on your wraps. I hope all of you have a wonderful Thanksgiving with your families." She smiled affectionately at them. "Class dismissed."

The children bustled out of the school and tore down the steps, scattering in all directions. But Annie didn't get far. There, at the bottom of the steps, sat Will, waiting for her in his buckboard.

She felt important and loved having such a handsome man picking her up. Two of the younger girls behind her blushed and tittered as they stared at Will with infatuation.

"Afternoon darlin'," Will greeted her with a loving smile. He hopped off the wagon and came toward her. "Thought you might like a ride home today."

A huge smile spread across Annie's face. "I sure would." Will took hold of her mittened hand and helped her up into the wagon beside him. They snuggled against each other as Will started off in the direction of the Allister home.

Although it was November, the sun was bright in the sky. For some time, Will and Annie drove in silence until Annie noticed that they were actually not headed toward her home.

"Will," Annie enquired curiously. "Where are we going?"

There was that mysterious sparkle in his eyes again. "We're taking the long way to your place," he answered.

Will stopped his wagon at the lake. The water looked dangerously cold. Annie shivered. She couldn't figure out what Will was up to, but before she knew it, they were looking at each other, longing for each other.

Their faces inched closer and closer until their lips met. Annie held Will with such an urgency that at first it frightened her, but then, she noticed Will was doing the same thing to her and it felt wonderful. She knew she wanted nothing more in the world at that moment.

The kiss lingered, and Annie groaned with pleasure as Will's hands paved their way up her spine.

Annie thought she might not want to stop, and it was Will who did first. It seemed to Annie as though he almost pushed her away. At first, she couldn't understand why he wanted to stop. Did she kiss wrong? Didn't he enjoy it as much as she did?

Will reached into the deep pocket of his wool coat and yanked out a beautiful shining silver ring. Annie was completely astonished. She thought her bottom lip was going to fall straight to the frozen ground.

"Annie," he said and looked at her with urgency, "I'm sure it's no secret that I've become quite fond of you these last several weeks." His face turned three different shades of red at this confession.

Annie nodded dazedly as he continued. "I guess you could say I've grown to … to love you. And it would make me the happiest man in the world if you would agree to be my wife." And with that, he slipped the ring onto her icy finger.

Her cheeks turned crimson. "Yes! Oh, Will, yes!"

Will laughed and said, "I can't tell if you're cold or blushing because of my question."

CHAPTER 12

Thanksgiving morning was a chaotic one in the Allister home. Mama had been awake since before sunup, already beginning to cook the important meal that was coming up later that day. Annie and Beth were also awake and lending a helping hand where needed. They were all excited for the day, and they all talked at once, even bumping into each other a few times. But they were all too overjoyed to care. And as soon as Pa finished hitching up the team, they were going to church.

It had been another beautiful and meaningful service, and the Allister family was ready for the wonderful meal that was waiting for them at home. Annie was especially anticipating this afternoon because she had invited Will and his family over.

The wagon rattled down the icy path leading to the Allister farm, and Beth's eyes suddenly grew wide. "Who's that?" she asked.

"Dunno," Pa said. None of them could make out the two figures huddled together in the lean-to.

"Land sakes," Mama gasped. She practically jumped out of the wagon and flew into the arms of her sister.

"Goodness, woman. Would you let me stop drivin' before you go leapin' out like that?" Pa scolded sternly.

But Mama and Aunt Frances were both too overjoyed to answer. The sisters exchanged greetings and tears, and everyone bustled into the house where they were immediately welcomed by the wonderful aroma of turkey.

Seeing Aunt Frances and Sam today was quite a shock. They were three days early. Annie hadn't spoken to Sam yet, but so far, she was amazed at what she saw. Sam was utterly flawless. She had long, golden hair and eyes as blue as a clear summer day. She was lean and tall, and when she smiled, Annie noticed that even her teeth were perfectly set. She looked like a porcelain doll.

"And so," Aunt Frances was in the middle of explaining, "we figured it would be alright to show up a few days early. I hope it's okay?"

Pa answered for Mama. "Of course it's okay. It's Thanksgiving. The more the merrier."

"Annie's beau is coming with his family," Beth chimed in.

"You have a beau?" Sam asked incredulously.

They were the first words out of Sam's mouth, and they left Annie feeling insulted, as if Sam couldn't believe Annie could possibly have a beau. Her back stiffened. "Why yes, I do," she answered matter-of-factly. Annie glared at her little sister for announcing it like that.

"And here they are now," Pa announced, starting toward the door. Annie's heart fluttered as it always did when Will was present.

John, Alice, and their two boys filed into the house, and Mama and Aunt Frances took their wraps and offered them some coffee. Finally, Will stepped inside, looking as dashing as ever.

He walked over to Annie and took her in his arms. "Hello, darlin'," he whispered in her ear, and they kissed lightly. The couple held hands as Pa introduced everyone.

When it was time for Sam's introduction, she glided right over to Will, put her hands on his hips, and boldly gave him a kiss on the cheek.

Annie was astounded that Sam would so boldly do that in front of her like that. Jealousy welled up inside of her. She decided then and there that she did not like Sam one bit, and she was determined to keep a close eye on her when Will was near.

"A pleasure to meet you," Sam drawled in Will's ear.

"Pleasure's all mine," Will said with a wide grin on his face. He took a good long look at Sam's beauty as she walked over to the table and sat down. Will followed and sat beside her, the two of them smiling at one another the entire time.

"Annie," Mama called, "I will need your help setting the table."

"Yes, ma'am," she obeyed. She went into the kitchen to start carrying the dishes to the table. Wild thoughts went through her head the entire time. Did Will enjoy the flirtatious attention Sam had given him? It certainly appeared that way. He seemed to forget Annie was present.

She set the places at the table as her mother had told her to, and she couldn't help but notice how consumed Will and Sam were with one another. She flinched when she heard them talking about how close in age they were, Will at twenty, and Sam, nineteen.

Everyone sat down at the table, and Pa said grace. Then, Mama's delicious meal she had worked so hard to prepare was devoured. There was much talking and laughing amongst the family members. But Annie was distracted by the fact that she had somehow become seated across the table from Will instead of beside him. Sam was still stuck to his arm, and Annie found it difficult to watch. She desperately hoped she would get the chance to spend some time with him later that afternoon.

And she did.

It was Beth's turn to help Mama in the kitchen, so Annie and Will sat comfortably beside each other by the fire. John and Pa discussed the latest crop prices, and Aunt Frances and Alice became acquainted.

Annie was worried because Alice hadn't said a word to her the entire time she'd been there. She hoped Alice liked her since they would be family someday.

"Your ma's meal was delicious," Will told her as she squeezed his hand affectionately. She agreed. "She always makes such good meals." She moved a bit closer to her beloved, and at that very moment, Sam bounded over to the sofa and sat down beside Will. The two smiled at each other.

Annie knew she would have to do everything she could to distract her cousin. "Are you still playing piano, Sam?"

Sam looked at her as if she had interrupted a very important conversation. "Yes," she replied sourly. She took a deep breath as she tried coming up with a good answer. "I still love to play, but our piano was destroyed in the fire. Now, I am no longer able to because I will be living here, amongst poor people with no piano."

Annie was appalled by that remark, but it instantly brought Alice to life. "Honey, we have a piano, and you can use it anytime you want to."

Sam clapped her dainty hands together excitedly. "Oh, I will, I will." She turned to Will and batted her eyelashes at him flirtatiously. "Will, honey, I do hope you will want to take me out to your place soon so I can use the piano."

Will looked uncomfortable for a moment and then replied, "I reckon I can." He cleared his throat nervously. "That way nobody can accuse me of being unfriendly." He looked at Annie uneasily as she glared at him. He hadn't even invited her out there yet, but after knowing Sam for only a few short hours, she had been invited by both Will and his sister-in-law.

And to make matters worse, Sam threw Annie a smug look as if to gloat about the attention Will gave her.

As the afternoon wore on, Sam and Alice talked to one another continuously. Beth was occupying Will's young nephews, and the other adults sat visiting at the kitchen table.

Annie and Will remained on the sofa, holding hands. "I have missed you so much these last few weeks," she confessed to him.

"I sure am sorry, Annie. I know I only came by twice in three weeks, but we've been real busy on the farm, and I needed to help."

"Oh." was the only thing she could think of as a reply. "Well, I can understand that." The two of them kissed shyly as Sam shot them a look of jealously.

* * *

Will began coming out to the Allister farm more often after he and Annie had talked on Thanksgiving, only now it seemed as though he divided his attention between both herself and Sam. His first visit since Thanksgiving began with him and Annie taking a walk up The Hill. It was bitterly cold, but Annie didn't mind one bit. She felt fine as long as she was with Will.

But when they walked back to the farm, there was Sam standing at the bottom, waiting for them. "Hello," she called out in a shrill voice. Her hand flew high above her head as she waved frantically.

She skipped over to the couple. "William, I thought maybe you could take me to your place so I could use your piano today." She fluttered her eyelids seductively at him.

Will was obviously uncomfortable at this and glanced nervously at Annie before answering, "Of course."

"Oh, good!" Sam screeched as she clapped her hands like a two-year-old. "So long, Annie," she said, and she linked her arm in Will's. He looked at her apologetically as he walked off with no kiss for her.

CHAPTER 13

The next day, Will dropped by again. Annie noticed him walking down The Hill when she happened to glance out the window. She ran outside to greet him. She had been wanting to discuss something with him, and this seemed like the perfect time to do it before Sam sunk her claws into him again.

They walked quietly to the house together and went in. "Sit down," Annie motioned to the table as they removed their wraps. "Would you like some coffee?" He nodded his head, and Annie brought two piping hot cups to the table. She sat down across from Will and gave him a hard stare. She silently thanked God the rest of her family had gone to the Wilson's for the afternoon for a visit. Annie had told her folks she was too tired to visit, which gave her the perfect opportunity to talk to Will privately.

She looked across the table at him, took a deep breath, and began. "Will, I need to talk to you about something that is very important."

He looked confused. "Sure. Go ahead."

She looked down at her hands as if that would somehow prevent them from shaking. "Will, I'm worried about your feelings for me."

If Will had looked confused before, he was even more so now. "What do you mean by that?" His eyes held a blank stare, and it annoyed her that she would have to explain it to him. She assumed this situation was blatantly obvious to the world.

She folded her hands in front of her. This was it. This was the moment that would determine the rest of her life. She took a deep breath before beginning. "Will, you seem to be awfully interested in my cousin," she explained. "Ever since the day she showed up, I have felt like I am sharing you with her."

Will did not seem surprised by what Annie had said at all, which meant she was right. Will knew he had been crossing the line. "I assure you, my darling, you are seeing something that isn't there. It's you I love, not her."

She felt like jumping out of her chair and screaming. "Oh, Will, I was hoping you'd say that!" She leaned across the table to kiss him, but he pushed her away, right in time.

"Watch out for the coffee!" he said with a chuckle as he saved it from spilling.

Later that evening as Annie stared at the ceiling above her bed, she felt much better. Perhaps what she saw between Will and Sam was just her wild imagination. From now on, she would have to ignore Sam's actions and concentrate on her future as Will's wife.

CHAPTER 14

Christmas came and went that year, much like Thanksgiving had, only this time, the Allister family were guests at the Montgomery home.

And after the holidays were over, the wind and snow were persistent, keeping mostly everyone indoors unless it was absolutely necessary to be outside. Annie and her family preferred the warmth of the indoors during the frigid winter, and only Sam ventured out once or twice a week to play piano at Will's place.

It had been two weeks since Annie had seen him. She missed him terribly, and since today was one of the days Sam was going over there, Annie asked her if she could give Will a message.

"Sam, could you please tell Will that I miss him and that he should come calling soon?" she asked politely.

"If I remember," Sam replied, absently shrugging her shoulders as she flounced out the door.

* * *

Pa's birthday was always a simple affair, as Pa preferred only cake and the three ladies in his life. Annie, Beth, and Mama spent the afternoon together baking his cake. It always had to be chocolate, his favorite. They always enjoyed their time baking together and had invited Aunt Frances to join them, but she just sat in Mama's rocking chair, knitting.

Beth looked over at her and wrinkled up her nose. "She doesn't seem to help out much around here," she whispered to her mother.

"No," Mama replied, "home affairs ain't her thing, I guess."

Annie had to agree. Since the day they showed up here, Aunt Frances and Sam did absolutely nothing. The Allisters gave them a home, food, and hospitality, and still, the two women were rude, unkind, and acted better than everyone around them, throwing their fancy clothing and lifestyles in everyone's faces. From that very first day, Annie had known without a doubt she would not like them. Now, she was sure of it.

The sky outside had turned a sinister shade of gray, and before long, huge snowflakes, all in different patterns, began to zig zag down from the angry clouds. No one inside seemed to notice. They were busy baking, and it was quite some time before Pa tramped in, covered in snow.

"Goodness Graham, you are a sight," Mama exclaimed.

Pa shook the snow off his clothes. "It's really coming down out there." He took off his wraps, hung them up, and wasted no time huddling in front of the fire.

Beth and Aunt Frances went to the window. "I hope Samantha has the good sense to stay the night at Will's place for the night," Frances said to Beth. "She oughta enjoy it plenty. She's had her eye on that boy from the moment she laid eyes on him."

Annie's heart sank when she heard that, and her mother gave her a concerned look. But Pa on the other hand nodded his head confidently. "She'll know better, believe me. You can't see your hand in front of your face."

Wickedly, Annie hoped Sam would be able to make it home, and it wasn't because she enjoyed her cousin's company. She didn't. Not at all. It was because she couldn't be trusted with Will. It was a horrible thought to have, but she couldn't help the way she felt.

As the evening wore on, the blizzard outside became more intense. The wind howled loudly, and tiny pellets of ice blasted against the windowpane. Pa stood in front of it and tried looking out of it, but to no avail. "Yup," he bellowed, "it's a blizzard alright."

Aunt Frances began sobbing. "My baby girl could be out in that mess!"

"Now Frances," Mama tried consoling her by taking her in her arms, "I'm sure she is safe at the Montgomery place."

And later, as the aroma of the beef stew filled the air in the cozy little farmhouse, the family ate their meal in silence. It was now obvious to everyone that Sam would not be coming home for the night. It was already pitch-black outside, and the blizzard, it seemed, had no intention of letting up any time soon.

Annie and Beth cleared the table, and Mama filled the kettle with water for fresh coffee. Pa had ventured out one last time for the evening to check the stock. He had put up an extra thick rope at the start of the storm extending from the barn to the house so he wouldn't get lost out in the blizzard.

While he was outside, the ladies worked on their knitting. Mama constantly had to darn Pa's socks and always insisted it was a relaxing job. Annie sat on the edge of Aunt Frances' bed, which was across from the table. The house had become quite crowded since the two houseguests moved in, but it was either here or find a home of their own, and Mama wouldn't hear of it.

Annie's mind was, of course, on Will. She worried that Sam's beauty would influence him to end his courtship with Annie and jump into a fresh romance with her cousin. After all, Will's attraction to Sam had been more than obvious from the day the two of them met. And Sam was lovely enough to have any man she wanted, but she loved to compete. It was exciting for her to chase after someone else's beau.

Annie bit her nails nervously, although she knew her mother would not approve if she saw it. She hoped and prayed that Will would use his common sense in Sam's presence. His future with Annie depended on it.

CHAPTER 15

There was much anticipation in the Allister home the next morning. The weather had greatly improved. There was no more howling wind, but rather a calm, barely noticeable whisper. The only remnants of the storm were the bone-chilling temperatures and two feet of snow.

Aunt Frances paced back and forth in front of the window overlooking the yard and, further in the distance, The Hill. She rubbed her hands together anxiously.

Annie, also anxious for Sam's return, but for a completely different reason, looked simply lovely in her gingham dress. She had purposely worn her good dress because she knew Will was coming, and she wanted to look pretty for him.

It seemed an eternity, but finally Will's sled could be spotted in the distance, slithering clumsily toward the Allister farm. "They're coming," announced Beth.

"Finally," Annie muttered under her breath. She and Aunt Frances scampered over to the window and anxiously peered out right as the sled came to a halt.

Will and Sam said good-bye to one another. Will helped Sam down from the wagon and the two held hands, then embraced. Then, Will pulled away, lifted Sam's chin, and kissed her passionately.

The kiss seemed to linger much too long, and Annie became furious. It was just like Sam to go after the man Annie was to marry soon.

Finally, Sam bounced into the house, snow spiraling down from her glistening yellow hair, her face shining.

"Samantha," Aunt Frances cried. "Oh, baby girl, I was so worried about you when the storm hit." She took her daughter in her arms in a protective embrace.

But Sam just laughed it off. "Oh, mother, no need to worry about me. I had an exquisite time."

That statement enraged Annie. She decided it was time to step in. "I'll bet you did," she shot back ferociously. She stepped right up in her cousin's face. "How dare you!" Her voice was much louder now.

Sam took a step back with innocence written all over her face. "Why, whatever do you mean, dear cousin?" Her eyelids fluttered, and her voice held a sugary tone.

"As if you don't know," Annie retorted. Her voice shook with anger. "You're trying to take my beau from me." She hoped her words would sink in and prompt Aunt Frances to do something about it.

Sam threw her head back and laughed a wicked laugh. "Poor Annie, let me fill you in. As of yesterday, William is no longer yours. He's mine now." Her beautifully wicked eyes glimmered triumphantly.

"You're lying," Annie accused through clenched teeth as she glared at her cousin.

Sam's baby blue eyes slanted with cruelty as she remarked, "Unfortunately for you, I am not lying. He said himself that he wants to be with me now instead of you." And when Annie stared at her incredulously, she taunted, "Go ahead. Ask him."

"I certainly will do just that," Annie's voice became louder by the minute. "Tomorrow. When he comes by to see me."

"You mean me," Sam grunted as she flounced away from her cousin. It was all Annie could do to keep from slapping Sam in her pretty little face. Instead, she marched into her room and slammed the door. Hard. She couldn't wait until tomorrow. She would prove to Sam and to everyone else as well that Sam was wrong about Will's friendliness toward her.

CHAPTER 16

The sun was shining brightly in the sky the next morning. Annie ate her breakfast, trying to avoid Sam the entire time. She helped Mama clear the table afterward, and as she stacked the dishes neatly beside the sink, she heard the familiar sound of Will's wagon coming up the road.

She quickly went to the door and let him in. He removed his wraps, and Annie couldn't help but notice that he and Sam exchanged endearing looks. Annie felt a huge lump forming in her throat. This was going to be more difficult than she thought. But she bravely cleared her throat and croaked out the words. "Will, please come into the bedroom with me. We need to have a serious talk."

Will looked down at his feet and shifted his body uncomfortably. He gave Sam a look of dread before following Annie into her tiny bedroom. He shut the door behind him and sat down on the bed. The sun was shining brightly through the window, leaving a slat of light across the floor.

Annie sat down on the bed beside Will. This was an important talk they were about to have, and she needed to focus. She took a deep breath and began. "I have been having my doubts lately about your feelings for me, and after some of the things Sam has told me, I need you to explain to me what is going on."

Will's eyes overflowed with guilt, and he struggled to look at Annie. His voice cracked. "Well, when Samantha was out at our place yesterday, she got on so good with the family. You know, she just kind of fit in." He scratched his eyebrow and hesitated before beginning again. "Then, when the storm hit and she had to stay over, we spread a blanket by the fire and talked. She told me that she wants to be a mother and be married to a farmer. She likes horses; she enjoys the quiet farm life. Plus, we have our age in common." He looked urgently at Annie, who said nothing. "And by the end of the evening, I decided she would be the right woman for me. I truly am sorry, Annie." He flashed her a look that was anything but sorry.

Annie could not believe what she had just heard. Was he really that stupid? "First of all," Annie fired back, tapping off each reason on her fingers, "I happen to know that none of the above is true. Sam has already said she would never marry a farmer. She wants to live in the big city, and she greatly dislikes horses. Pa can't even get her to step foot in the barn to fetch something for him." She was standing up by now with her hands on her hips, glaring angrily at him.

But Will had also become quite angry as well. His eyes held a fiery tint. "What are you trying to say, Annie? That Samantha is lying?"

"Yes," she shouted at him. "Yes. Don't you see? Sam is always going after things she can't have. She finds it appealing to chase after you knowing that we are to be married." She took Will's hand in her own and said in a gentler voice, "I love you, Will, and I happen to want you for all the right reasons." She smiled up hopefully at him, thinking he might kiss her, hoping he would realize how wrong he was, and everything would be okay again.

But Will's back stiffened, and he stood up, unable to face her. His voice held no feeling as he admitted her worst fears to her. "I'm sorry, Annie, but I want Samantha now."

His hand dropped from hers, and once again, she felt the anger rising inside of her. "Does this have anything to do with how beautiful she is?" she asked him, although she already knew the answer.

Will's cheeks turned a bright crimson. He hesitated, afraid to admit the truth but knowing he had to. She deserved that much from him. "Well, every man wants a woman who looks like Samantha. With her beauty, I know that she will always be able to satisfy me after a hard day of work."

Unbelievable, Annie thought angrily. Was he actually dumb enough to choose beauty over love? She threw her arms up in the air in disgust. "Fine," she said. It was all she could do to remain calm. Her lips trembled, and she was absolutely furious. "I don't know what I ever wanted with you in the first place. I mean, I wanted the simple things in life. Children, a man to love, a happy home life. I thought you were the perfect man, but obviously, I was so very wrong. Those things are just too boring for you, aren't they, Will?" By now, the tears streamed down her face. "You don't want any of the things that matter in life." It startled her to hear herself say that, but she was so angry.

"Annie, please," Will pleaded. "We should talk about this more."

"No!" she shouted. "You made your decision. There's nothing more to talk about. Now get out of my room." She feverishly twisted and pulled on the engagement ring that had adorned her dainty hand. Once it came off, she threw it at him.

He picked it up on his way out the door. "Don't say I didn't warn you," she shouted to him right as the door closed behind him.

Annie took a deep breath, wiped the tears from both cheeks, and flung her body down onto her bed. Never in all her sixteen years had she cried as hard or as much as she did that very moment. She had lost the first love of her life, and it felt as though someone had taken a knife to her heart. Her entire body shook uncontrollably with anger.

Annie cried for what seemed an eternity. She was so distraught that no thoughts went through her head at all. It was as though she was the only human being on the planet. And she jumped when she felt a hand resting gently on her shoulder. It was her mother, eager to console her heartbroken daughter.

Sitting up on her bed, she threw herself into her mother's arms and stayed there until she had no more tears to shed.

When the two women finished embracing, Annie grabbed her soft pink handkerchief off the bedside table and wiped her tears one last time. "Oh, Mama," she wailed, her voice broken, "it hurts so much. What do I do?" She turned to her mother with pleading eyes. She knew her mother would help her.

"I'm so sorry, dear," came Mama's surprising answer, "but the two of them have made a choice, and I'm afraid there's nothing we can do about it." Lillian Allister felt her daughter's obvious pain, for she, too, had suffered a similar heartbreak many years before.

It was the worst thing her mother could've said to her, yet deep in her heart, Annie knew it was true. Ultimately, the choice was to be made by Will and Sam. Still, she felt like a little girl again, needing her mother's protection. She snuggled up in the crook of her mother's arm. More tears welled up in her eyes, and her voice shook with agony as she searched for an answer to her painful dilemma. "How do I make it stop hurting?"

Mrs. Allister squeezed her daughter tighter, saying reassuringly, "Honey, I know you don't believe this right now, but time will heal your heart. You will forget about this one day. You will move on with your life, and you will find another man to love, one who will realize what a gem you are. One who will treat you right."

"Do you think so?" Annie asked with both hope and uncertainty in her voice.

"I really do," Mama answered.

And something about the sureness in her mother's voice made Annie believe it too.

PART TWO
Sam and Will

CHAPTER 17

Spring boldly arrived at the Allister farm with huge piles of snow thawing rapidly into puddles of murky water. There was mud everywhere, and all of the trees and miles of grass anxiously awaited being born again.

Annie's thin shawl covered her shoulders as she strolled down the saturated road on her way home from Margaret's place. She had been spending as much time with her friend as possible. Although she had begun to feel a little bit better after the breakup with Will, she still found it difficult to be at home.

It seemed to Annie that every waking moment was spent discussing or planning the upcoming wedding between Will and Sam. She was almost certain the very moment Will left her room that day that he immediately went and proposed marriage to Sam. The two of them had spoken to Pa and Aunt Francis about building a home nearby, and Pa said he'd be glad to do it, but he couldn't guarantee it would be finished in time for the wedding.

Aunt Francis, who had the knack of saying the wrong thing at the absolute worst time, put her two cents worth in. "Well, that don't matter, Graham. The answer is right here under our noses." She looked ready to burst at any moment. "There's no reason why they can't just stay in Sam's room until they have their own place."

Mama winced and spoke right up. "Now Francis, I don't think that's the best idea. It's already plenty crowded in there."

"Yes," Pa added, "Annie has sacrificed enough of her room already." He thought a moment. "Will, could the two of ye stay at your brother's place until the house is built?"

"Oh no, sir," Will answered with absolute certainty. "There are already four people living in that one-bedroom house." He turned and looked longingly at his future bride, who planted a huge kiss on his lips.

The room fell silent as everyone tried to come up with some other idea.

Suddenly, Pa shook his head and turned to look at Annie, who had been silently listening to the conversation. "I'm sorry, honey," he said to her, his eyes filled with empathy for her, "but we have no choice. We simply can't afford to put them up in a hotel for such a length of time, and I know Montgomery can't either. They will have to stay here."

Annie felt as if someone had ripped out all of her insides with tweezers. Her pa was supposed to be on her side. She felt as though the whole world was betraying her lately. "No," she cried in despair. She waited a moment while she studied the different facial expressions of her family members. It was obvious from the helpless, pained look in their eyes that her parents understood. Beth's face was expressionless, as though she would rather be anywhere else than witnessing this discussion. Annie didn't blame her one bit. Aunt Frances, Sam, and Will, on the other hand, looked confused, almost as though they couldn't understand Annie's rejection.

She continued. "Do you think it's easy for me to be in the same room with those two every day? No. I can't stand seeing them kissing, hugging, cuddling. And now, you expect me to sleep in the same room with the man who broke my heart into a million pieces, seeing him sleep with another woman?"

But Pa held firm. "I'm sorry, honey, but there is no other way to go about it." Aunt Frances is already sleeping out here. And since you and Beth have the biggest room in the house, you all will have to adjust to sharing a room."

Annie was absolutely mortified. Her room was already crowded enough with Beth and Sam in it. The room was divided in half by a sheet with Annie and Beth on one side and Sam on the other.

She knew it was useless to continue arguing. Everyone else seemed to approve of the decision.

And so, it was settled. She had no choice but to endure the pain of seeing Will in Sam's arms the moment she woke up. And it would be incredibly horrifying to have to listen to the intimate sounds the two lovers were sure to make. She shuddered just thinking about it.

CHAPTER 18

The wedding day, set for early May, quickly approached. Everyone had their own suggestions about the color of the flowers, how she should wear her hair, and every detail pertaining to the wedding. But of course, Sam wanted to be in charge, and although her mother and everyone around her were trying to help, Sam snapped at every person who tried to give her any advice. Lily Allister had shrugged her shoulders and said under her breath to Annie, "It is her special day. I suppose it's best to just let her be."

The wedding was to be held in the tiny church in town with Reverend Johnston marrying the young couple. It would be a small ceremony with the families of both the bride and the groom and the Wilsons attending.

John had the honor of being the groomsman and Margaret, for reasons Annie could not understand, would be the bridal attendant. Annie remembered the precise moment Margaret had told her about it. She had been visiting the Wilson home doing nothing in particular that day except avoiding her own family. It was upsetting news, but Margaret had assured her she had said yes to Sam only to be polite.

The wedding was only three days away, and there seemed to be an unusual amount of chaos present in the Allister home of late. Annie was almost certain Sam tried on her gown at least once a day. It was a lavish, white, flowing gown with lace-trimmed sleeves. A smooth ribbon enveped the waist of it, and the top half generously accentuated Sam's stunning curves. Sam's mother had worn that same dress on her wedding day, and it was one of the few items Aunt Frances saved when the great fire broke out.

Mama and Aunt Frances frantically prepared the meals for that day, and Pa and Will rearranged the girls' bedroom to make room for another set of drawers.

And at last, the day Annie had been dreading arrived. It was an early hour, but a hint of perfection hung in the air. The sun was just coming up, and the birds surrounding the farmhouse sang happily.

The Allister household was in a frenzy. They spent the morning bathing, dressing in their best clothing, and eating a light lunch before piling into Pa's wagon and heading into town. The families of the couple arrived at the church an hour before the service. The womenfolk were in the reverend's little room making quite a fuss over Sam. They helped her into her gown and told her repeatedly how exquisite she looked. And Sam enjoyed every minute of it.

Even Annie had to admit Sam looked exceptional. Nothing about Sam was flawed today. She was absolutely stunning to look at. And Annie was absolutely positive that was Will's main reason for marrying her. He had been infatuated with her appearance since the minute he met her. Annie knew it wasn't Sam's personality he fell in love with. She was a rude, impatient young lady who always had to have her way.

Annie truly hoped Will would be happy with Sam. She still cared deeply for him and didn't want to see him hurt.

The bride was glowing, and the groom was proud, not only of his soon-to-be wife but also proud of the way his life had turned out up to this point. The daffodils were lovely in Mrs. Wilson's delicate vase. Aunt Frances wore a radiant smile, and the other guests were all in place. Everything looked perfect. The ceremony began.

The wedding was beautiful, even though Annie was hurting. She wished she could trade places with her cousin. She desperately wished she was the one walking down that aisle to profess her love to Will.

It didn't take long for Reverend Johnson to exclaim, "I now pronounce you man and wife. You may kiss the bride." And Will certainly did not hesitate. He and Sam kissed, then gaily headed down the aisle and out of the church.

And that was that. Will Montgomery was now officially a married man.

Everyone filed out of the church, chattering excitedly and congratulating the newly married couple, then heading straight to the Allister farm. Mama and Aunt Frances had a celebration planned, with delicious food and refreshing lemonade. There were blankets spread out on the ground to sit on. Pa took most of the guests to see the progress of the house. Everyone had asked questions, and it was only a mile away. The guys had been working on it every day for quite some time and nobody had actually gone out that way to see it. Everyone piled into Pa's wagon, and as soon as it was out of sight, Margaret came over and sat down on the blanket beside Annie. They were both silent for a moment before Margaret spoke. "Earth to Annie," she said as she waved the palm of her hand up and down in front of Annie's eyes. "You look like you are a million miles away right now."

Annie flashed her friend a fake smile. "I wish I was. I feel so out of place right now. Everyone is so happy and having a great time. But not me. I feel like everyone has forgotten the pain I still feel every time I see him."

Sympathy filled Margaret's eyes, and she patted Annie's hand gently. "I know, honey. But I haven't forgotten. And I'm concerned about you. So, if you ever need to talk, I will always be here for you."

Annie was grateful for her beautiful, loving friend. "Thank you, Margaret."

"And I want to apologize one last time for agreeing to be Sam's bridesmaid. You know I don't like her one bit, but it just isn't like me to be rude. So, when she asked me, I said yes."

Annie appreciated her friend's honesty. "I know." She hesitated before continuing. "You know, Margaret, she just makes me so mad sometimes. It almost seems like she is taking all of the people I love and care about away from me."

"Well, one thing is for sure," Margaret said with absolute certainty, "she will not take me away from you."

The two young ladies exchanged tender smiles right as Pa's wagon returned.

Everyone tried talking all at the same time. They were all pleased with what they had seen. Alice and Mama began discussing where the garden should be planted, and Mrs. Wilson generously offered to sew some curtains for the windows.

The festive party continued well into the evening with John playing his fiddle and everyone dancing and clapping their hands. It didn't take long for dusk to arrive, and Annie felt more alienated than ever. She decided she had had enough. She walked over to Mama and said, "I'm really tired. I think I'll go to bed now." She yawned for the hundreth time.

Mama looked up at her eldest daughter and stood up to hug her. "That's fine, dear. And listen, I want you to know how proud of you I am. I know how difficult this whole day has been for you, yet you handled it like a mature adult. Good night, sweetheart."

"Good night, Mama, and thank you." She placed a kiss on her mother's cheek, headed for the house, and entered her bedroom. After slipping into her night clothes, she crawled into bed and curled up underneath the blankets. The nights were still chilly, and Annie was unable to stop her teeth from chattering noisily. She wished sleep would come to her soon so she wouldn't be awake when Sam and Will came in, but she could not fall asleep. Her mind constantly recalled the troubled look in Sam's eyes when they came back from looking at the house.

Poor Will, she thought. Sam probably wasn't happy about living in such a simple little home. She wanted a fancy home in the city, complete with elegant lace curtains and even a parlor. And that was something Will simply could not provide.

Finally, Annie's mind settled down, and she began to doze off, only to be awakened by whispering voices and giggles outside the bedroom door. She noticed the music outside had stopped, which indicated the party was over. Listening silently, Annie heard the door click shut, followed by the sounds of Will and Sam kissing urgently.

Annie was not sure why, but for some reason, she crawled out of bed and crept over to the sheet that divided the room. The moonlight provided just enough light for her to see the two newlyweds begin consummating their marriage, and she found it impossible to stop watching.

Soon after they had shut the door behind them, they wasted no time. Their kissing continued, Sam moaning with desire. They quickly made their way to the freshly made bed, and their bodies intertwined clumsily.

Annie knew what was about to happen, and a huge lump formed in her throat. She could not watch anymore and tip-toed back to her bed. Tears rolled down her cheeks. It was true that Will was married now, but Annie still felt hurt and betrayed, knowing she could've been the one Will made love to. And she cried because of the unfamiliar feeling rising inside of her, tingling from head to toe. She had never felt anything like it before, and she couldn't do anything to make it go away. It made her long for a man, any man, to be in her bed, replaying with her the scenario she had just witnessed.

CHAPTER 19

Eggs. Two dozen of them. Large, small, brown, white, floating around in her head. They smelled like nothing she had ever smelled before. They smelled absolutely delicious. Glorious. Annie stirred in her sleep and, realizing it was Mama's breakfast she was smelling, woke up and stretched. She went over to her slim mirror to get dressed and brush her long hair, which was always a bit tangled after a long night of sleep. Her eyes were puffy from the broken sleep she had just woken up from.

She gave herself a good hard glare and knew that no matter how beautiful Sam was, Annie would be the better person. And then, the anguish washed over her as she recalled the steamy love scene she had witnessed just hours earlier.

Annie couldn't help but wonder what kind of wife and mother her cousin would be. Sam freaked out at the mere sight of dirt, and she always refused to do dishes or even take the kettle off the stove, let alone cook anything.

But what mystified her the most was what Sam would do when their first child arrived. She didn't have a kind bone in her body. How would she treat a small child?

She set her hairbrush down once again on the bureau and went out to the kitchen where Mama had already begun serving breakfast. Annie's appetite was enormous this morning, and she wasted no time filling up her plate with Mama's eggs and bacon and pouring herself some fresh milk.

Everyone had already been at the table before Annie except the newly married couple. And everyone had dark circles under their eyes. *They're probably tired because they heard the same thing I had heard throughout the night*, Annie thought bitterly.

And just like that, they exited the bedroom and sat down at the table. Annie caught the ecstatic smile Sam threw in her mother's direction and once again felt jealousy return and surge through her entire body.

"Good morning, you two," Mama greeted them cheerfully, setting dishes in front of both of them.

"Sleep well last night?" Pa inquired, his eyes twinkling in Will's direction.

"It was incredible," Sam answered, which set Will's cheeks on fire, and everyone soon realized Sam was not referring to sleep at all.

Pa rubbed his chin mischievously and remarked, "I reckon we will have little ones running all over the place before we know it."

Sam wrinkled her nose upon hearing that. "Uncle Graham, please. That is the very last thing I want."

Will stared at her incredulously. "Well, I dunno about that. I'd kinda like three myself."

"We shall discuss it another time, William," she snapped at him.

"Yes," Aunt Frances agreed, "you can discuss it another time." She looked her daughter square in the eyes and gently patted her hand. "Honey, I'm sure Will ain't gonna make you do anything you don't wanna do."

Annie was disgusted. She had seen this behavior in her cousin since the day they arrived. It was a shame Will couldn't see past the tempting beauty to see what the real Sam was like.

But despite Sam's objections about motherhood, it was too late. The constant lovemaking between the two had indeed produced a new life, for Sam soon became ill.

She began vomiting in the mornings and was unable to eat breakfast. Nobody thought anything of it until Sam fainted one Sunday in church. Aunt Frances went out of her head with worry.

"Don't fret, Frances," Mama said as she put her arms around her sister's shoulders later that evening. "We can take her in to see Dr. Woods tomorrow, first thing."

"Yes, I suppose," Aunt Frances agreed, her eyes red and puffy from all the crying she had been doing.

"I'm sure it's nothing too serious," Mama tried consoling her.

Sam wiped away her own tears and chimed in, "Yes mother, I agree with Aunt Lillian. I probably just have the flu or something. I'm sure it will go away."

* * *

The early summer sun beat down on Annie's face as she fastened the last of Pa's work shirts securely on the clothesline to dry. Looking up, she saw Sam and Aunt Frances on top of The Hill approaching her.

For a moment, Annie was startled. Today had been Sam's visit to the doctor. From the look of the body language of the two women, Annie guessed they were upset. As much as she despised her cousin, she didn't want anything bad to happen to her.

Frances and Sam approached the house, and Annie followed them inside. Aunt Frances bluntly announced, "She's havin' a baby."

Mama looked shocked for a second, then embraced Sam excitedly. "Oh, sweetie!" she squealed. "What wonderful news! I'm so happy for you!"

But Frances didn't share her sister's enthusiasm. Her mouth was set in a straight line. There was a fierce look in her eyes. "I just can't believe the boy did it. My Samantha has no interest in young'uns." She paced the tiny kitchen area feverishly.

Meanwhile, Sam sat down at the kitchen table, frowning. It was obvious she was upset, and Annie felt like laughing out loud. Normally, this would be a happy occasion, yet Sam and her mother were acting like children. What did they expect would happen when a husband and wife share endless passion every night?

Annie did not feel sorry for her cousin in the least but instead felt tremendous joy for Will. She knew how badly he had wanted to be a father.

It didn't take long for Pa and Will to burst into the house. They had been working on Will's house all morning, and they were sweaty and dirty. Concern clouded Will's dark eyes the moment he spotted his forlorn wife seated at the kitchen table. He knelt beside her and wrapped his muscular arms around her frail body. "Whatever is the matter, my darling? What did the doctor have to say?"

Her icy voice answered, "I'm havin' a baby, William." She looked as though she was trying to hold back tears.

Will was speechless for a moment as he allowed the news to sink in. "Praise the Lord above," he hollered and threw his hat in the air. He hugged Pa heartily. "I'm gonna be a Papa." His voice quivered as tears formed in his eyes.

Everyone was anxious for the new baby, who would arrive in early February. Once Beth heard the news, she immediately began sewing a quilt for the baby. She took great care picking out delicate pink, yellow, and blue blocks of fabric from Mama's sewing box. Even Aunt Frances had softened to the idea of becoming a grandmother. She tried desperately to convince her daughter of the joys her child would bring to her.

But it was useless.

Over the next few months, summer came to an end, and fall was once again evident with its brilliant shades of orange and yellow decorating the landscape for miles.

And with the changes in the weather also came changes in the family. Sam struggled daily with her challenging role as a wife. Mama insisted on helping her learn how to cook and keep house, but Sam wasn't easy to teach. She wrinkled her nose at the mere mention of putting her delicate hands in a sink full of dirty dishes. And she was always cross, snapping at anyone who dared cross her path. And with the bulge under her dress growing larger each week, it seemed, it was a perfect excuse for her to stay off her feet while everyone else took care of the home and did the daily chores.

Sam and Will seemed to argue everyday about the smallest things. However, that didn't put the fire out in their bed. Every single night, they made passionate love, and neither of them seemed to care that the rest of the house knew it.

On those nights when sleep would not come for her, Annie would lie awake in her bed thinking about Will. The feelings she had once felt for Will had faded away. Now, her feelings for him were neutral. She didn't dislike him; however, she wasn't sure she particularly liked him anymore either.

Shortly after their breakup, Annie began to notice that Will wasn't as brilliant as she had once thought he was. And he certainly had only one thing on his mind. She knew that for sure as she had no choice but to listen, once again, to him and his wife making love. Annie really hoped their home would be finished soon. She didn't know how much more she could take.

Three days later, God answered her prayers when Pa and Will burst into the house with glorious smiles spread across their grubby faces. "What's going on with you two?" Beth asked suspiciously, looking up from the bread she was kneading.

"All finished," Pa announced proudly.

"The house?" Mama asked hopefully.

"The house. We put the last of the cupboards in just now."

And that was the end of Sam and Will living with the Allisters. The two of them didn't own much for belongings, so the next morning, bright and early, the moving process began.

Shawls were required that morning since the chilly weather had once again returned. The entire family piled into Pa's wagon and headed for the new house.

When they arrived and Annie had the chance to take in all that she saw, she was very impressed with it. It was a simple little home with thick, sturdy logs holding it together. It even had glass windows, which was a special request of Sam's.

Annie always knew Pa could do wonderful things with his hammer and some nails, but she didn't know to what extent until she stepped inside.

There were shelves on top of and on both sides of the fireplace. The kitchen cabinets had bold patterns meticulously carved on the fronts of them. There were two tiny bedrooms, one on each side of the house.

After careful examination of the entire house, both Pa and Will received hearty compliments for their work from everyone except Sam. She stood quietly by the fireplace, her hands clasped in front of her, a look of distaste spread across her face, although everyone else was too excited to notice or even care.

"Samantha darling," Aunt Frances said sweetly, "I bet your Aunt Lillian would love to help you put your belongings away."

Although Lillian was perfectly capable of speaking for herself, she graciously agreed. "I certainly would, Sam."

But Sam wouldn't hear of it. "No," she insisted in her aunt's direction. "We don't have much, so it won't take much to put it away."

Mama shrugged. "If you insist, darlin'. But I want you to know that if you ever need me to help out with anything, you just give a holler."

"I will," she promised and gave her aunt a false hug.

Everyone headed for home then, leaving Will and Sam behind in their new home.

For the first time since Sam and her mother had arrived, Annie was glad to be at home. Normalcy had returned to the household. *Now, if we could only ship Aunt Frances somewhere*, Annie thought wickedly, not caring how nasty and evil her thoughts were.

CHAPTER 20

The weather was brutally cold over the Christmas holiday, and Will and Sam rarely visited because of it. Sam's belly had become enormous, and it was just too much of a hassle to struggle putting on her wraps.

It was late afternoon on the third day of February. The sky was gray with the promise of a fresh layer of snow coming soon. Mama and Pa were in town running errands, and Beth and Annie were preparing beef stew for supper. They heard the frantic gallop of a horse outside, and before they could see who was approaching, Will burst into the house. He was out of breath, and his usually happy eyes were filled with fright.

Annie wiped her hands on a dish towel. She was frightened by the look in his eyes. "What's wrong?"

"The baby," he panted, "is coming."

Annie and Beth looked frantically at one another. "Beth," Annie ordered sternly, "wake up Aunt Frances." Beth obeyed her sister and ran urgently into her folks' bedroom where Frances had begun napping regularly because, according to her, there was too much traffic where her bed was.

Beth returned instantly with her aunt close at her heels.

"Please come with me, Annie," Will pleaded. "I could really use your support."

"Certainly," she replied. She turned to her sister. "Beth, stay here and tell Mama and Pa what's happening." Annie began bundling up as Will addressed his mother-in-law. "Mrs. Wilson is coming by to take you to our place."

Will and Annie rushed out to his waiting horse. He took her gloved hand in his and helped her up. She wrapped her arms around his waist and instantly felt a warm sensation inside of her. It was easy to see why Sam wanted Will as badly as she did. It was the same reason Annie herself had at one time. Will was a beautiful man.

She gave him an extra squeeze, although she knew he hadn't noticed. He was far too concerned about his wife and coming child.

It didn't take long to arrive, despite the horse's difficulty battling some of the high snow drifts.

Will jumped off the animal's back and left Annie sitting there. And although she didn't need help getting off, she couldn't help but feel somewhat insulted.

With a sigh, she hopped off the horse and raced to the house. She threw off her wraps the minute she was inside. The sky was already turning dark, and she could smell the kerosene Will had put in the lanterns.

Unsure why, Annie felt scared. She cautiously peeked into the bedroom where she saw Sam on the bed with her head propped up uncomfortably by two pillows. Annie had to turn away. She went to the stove and began boiling water. That was all she knew about childbirth. She prayed to God Aunt Frances and Mrs. Wilson would hurry. Sam would need someone in the room with her as she delivered her child.

The door flew open minutes later. Rosy-cheeked Aunt Frances cried, "Where's my baby?" She ran to the bedroom without waiting for the answer.

Mrs. Wilson, who would be delivering the child, remained calm and immediately took charge.

Annie entered the bedroom and stood at the back of the room with Will. She stole a glance at him. His beautiful eyes overflowed with concern. As if sensing her eyes on him, he met her glance and smiled nervously. A chill shot down Annie's spine. Will could still excite her even though he was now off-limits.

The hours passed, and it had long since turned dark. The only light was the dim lantern that had been lit. Annie's parents arrived with the dark. Aunt Frances continued sitting beside her daughter, comforting her. Mama began assisting Mrs. Wilson by keeping everyone calm and handing wet washrags to Frances for Sam's forehead.

Sam experienced horrific pain, and she screamed out as the agony intensified. Mama stood up from where she was kneeling at the foot of the bed and turned to the spectators. Her solemn eyes made her look very much in control as she ordered, "Every one of you needs to leave the room. Now. Leah will be checking Sam's progress again, and I have no doubt the birth will happen in a matter of minutes."

On his way out, Will stopped by the bed and bent to tenderly kiss his wife on her sweaty forehead. "I love you, baby," he whispered to her.

"I love you, too," she whispered back. She was out of breath from all of the intense breathing and pushing she had been doing.

"C'mon darlin'," Leah Wilson coaxed as she tried to pry Sam's legs apart. "I need to have a look so I know if it's time to push."

Sam eased her legs apart, and Leah exclaimed, "Land sakes, it's time all right. The baby's head is right there."

"Okay, honey," Mama coached, holding Sam's hand tightly in her own, "I know this is scary, but if you'll just do whatever Mrs. Wilson tells you to, it will all be over with soon, and you'll have a beautiful child in your arms."

Sam shot Mama a worried look, then let out a loud scream and grabbed a fistful of bedding. "Help me," she cried out.

Mrs. Wilson looked her square in the eyes. "Now, Samantha, it's time to push. As I'm counting to ten, you will have to bear down as hard as you possibly can, up to ten, take a quick breath and repeat. Ready?"

Sam nodded, and the birthing process began. She pushed only four times before Leah exclaimed, "It's a beautiful baby girl. You have a daughter, Samantha."

Mama's eyes filled with tears when she heard the announcement. Aunt Frances had long since been crying. But Sam seemed to have no emotion at all. She turned her head away and closed her eyes, refusing to hold the howling newborn who was desperate for her mother's touch.

The eager family members waiting outside were let back in the room. Will went straight to his wife, eyes wide and brimming with tears. He took hold of her hand and kissed it.

Leah Wilson walked around to the other side of the bed where Will sat. "Say hello to your daughter, William." She placed the child in her father's arms.

Will's amazement was obvious. "A daughter," he whispered, then turned to his wife. "She's beautiful, honey." He was crying, and Annie felt as though she may start to cry as well. She was overjoyed for Will. As she stood in the back of the room, she couldn't help but think how lovely the two parents looked with their new child. They were picture perfect.

It was well past midnight when the Allister family arrived back home. They were all exhausted but found it difficult to sleep from the earlier excitement. Mama warmed up some milk for everyone to drink, and soon, they all settled in their beds and got the good night of sleep they so desperately needed.

PART THREE
James

CHAPTER 21

The weather over the next few months turned out to be one of the nicest springs Annie could remember. The snow thawed almost as quickly as it had come, and the temperatures were warm enough to be enjoyable.

Annie, Beth, Aunt Francis, and Mama frequently walked over to Will and Sam's place to take them a cake or freshly baked bread. It also gave them the opportunity to see Emily Frances. She was a beautiful baby who, at only a few months old, seemed to be growing overnight. She had doubled her birth weight, and her chubby, rosy cheeks were enough to melt even Pa's heart.

Another change had happened in town. The mercantile had been sold to a family from up north. The previous owners were an elderly couple who couldn't manage it any longer. Their health had been deteriorating, and since their children were grown and moved away, they felt it was best to let someone else take over.

Annie couldn't wait to meet the new family. Everyone who already lived in town were dear friends, but it would be nice to see some new faces.

It turned out that she wouldn't have to wait long. She grabbed her shawl off the hook and said hastily over her shoulder, "Bye, Mama. I'm taking the eggs to town now." She picked up the basket on her way out the door.

The weather was almost perfect. The sun was bright, and the tall grass whispered in the warm breeze. Gregory was bustling with activity. It seemed everyone Annie had ever met was out and about for whatever reason.

She stopped short in front of her destination. The new owners had taken over only four days ago, and they were already having a sign put up that read, "Martin's Mercantile," painted in bright red letters.

Skipping up the creaky steps, she entered the quaint store. Upon looking around, she noticed that although most of it had been kept the same, a few small changes had begun. New, delicate curtains were hung on the windows, and a section of books had been added to one corner.

Awestruck, she walked over to look at them. There had never been books to purchase in the little town of Gregory before, and she knew a few people who would be excited about this, herself included.

A skinny woman with gray hair entered from the back room. "Hello, miss," she greeted loudly, making Annie jump.

"Oh, hello," Annie replied meekly.

"Another new face," the woman seemed to be saying to herself. She held out her hand and shook Annie's. "Well, I've been meeting so many new people, but I know I haven't met you yet. I'm Evelyn Martin."

Annie knew at once she would like Mrs. Martin. "I'm Annie Allister. My mother and father are Graham and Lily Allister. We live on a farm just a few miles from here. Oh, and I have a sister named Beth."

Evelyn Martin looked up from the shelf she was dusting off. "Well, Annie, I look forward to meetin' your family," she said with a friendly smile.

Annie smiled right back. "You'll like them." She wasn't sure what else to say, and she was about to turn around and venture back home when she remembered why she was there in the first place. "Oh," she exclaimed, "I almost forgot." She set the basket of eggs on the counter in front of Mrs. Martin. "Here are my mother's eggs."

Without saying a word, Mrs. Martin picked it up and began silently counting the eggs.

At that moment, Annie heard a scuffling noise from the back room. She turned to look and saw someone sweeping. He was a tall, young man, not much older than Annie herself. He had deep blue eyes and was very good looking.

"James," Mrs. Martin called to him, and the young man stopped sweeping and looked up. "Come and meet Annie."

He walked toward the two women, and as he did, Annie's stomach twisted in knots. She was immediately captivated by him and wanted desperately to know more about him.

His mother wasted no time with introductions. "Son, this is Annie Allister. Annie, this is my son, James." Annie shyly extended her hand to him and they shook hands.

James spoke first. "Pleased to meet you, Annie Allister." His voice was strong, and he sounded so confident and sure of himself.

"Likewise" was all Annie's mouth could produce.

He smiled then, and that made him all the more handsome. "Maybe I'll see you around sometime," he said to her.

"I'd like that," Annie replied, and she meant it. Although they had only just met, Annie felt the same way she had felt the day she met Will.

She snapped out of her thoughts in time to see James reaching up to a high shelf to grab something for his mother. "Thank you, Jimmy," Mrs. Martin said to her son, patting his arm lovingly.

"Ma," he said impatiently, "it's James."

But she ignored him and said, "You best go on and see if your pa needs more help."

"Yes, ma'am," he said obediently. He glanced over at Annie and waved. "See you next time."

She waved back. "Bye." And with that, he was gone. Now it was only her and Mrs. Martin, and since her business in the mercantile was finished, she decided it was time to go.

"I guess I'll be seeing you, Mrs. Martin. Welcome to town," she said politely, picking up the brown basket she had brought the eggs in.

"I'm sure you will," the older woman agreed. "Stop in to visit anytime."

"Thank you, ma'am. Good day."

"Good day, Annie."

Annie turned and walked out of the store and headed toward home. And from that moment and all throughout Mama's supper of delicious beef stew, biscuits, and fresh apple pie, all Annie thought about was James, the young man she had been so drawn to earlier that day.

Will, Sam, and Emily took supper with the Allisters that evening. That had been happening a lot lately, as Sam made it very clear that she disliked cooking, and Mama felt sorry for Will and Emily.

As soon as the apple pie had been served, Pa spoke up. "You certainly outdid yourself with this meal, Lil. Delicious!"

Mama looked at him lovingly. "Thank you, honey." The deep love between the two of them was evident by the looks they exchanged, and when Annie looked over at Will and Sam, she saw something entirely different. Sam sat on Will's lap with his hand clutching her thigh. He still had that dreamy, love-sick look in his eyes, but lately, Sam just seemed to be scowling.

Apparently, everyone else had noticed as well, because as Mama took Sam's plate away, she asked her, "What's the matter, honey? You don't look too happy."

Sam grunted. "I'm not happy at all. I saw the doctor today. Can you believe I'm havin' another baby?" Her nose wrinkled in disgust.

"Good Lord," Aunt Frances cried. "William, how could you do this to her? You know she wants to be a famous musician someday and can't be tied down with children her whole life." It looked as though she was going to smack Will, and Annie was worried for him.

But Will was offended. "As I told my wife earlier today, I am thrilled with the news, and I will help her with the two children whenever I can."

That seemed to pacify Aunt Frances somewhat. "I certainly hope so," she grumbled to no one in particular.

Again, the family waited over the months for the new baby. It was May again, which brought Will and Sam's one-year wedding anniversary.

And as spring vanished into summer, Annie found herself making excuses to go to town whenever Mama had an errand to run. No matter what business she had there, she always ended up at the mercantile. She was in luck most days when James was there, and he always made the time to talk to her. They quickly became friends, and Annie soon felt she was falling in love with him.

She and James began spending time together elsewhere, too, not only at the mercantile. Some days he would show up at the Allister farm and take Annie for long walks down the dirt road. They enjoyed the time they spent together laughing and talking.

On one of those particularly enjoyable walks, Annie noticed they were going right past Will's house. Annie pointed to it. "That's where Will and

Sam live." James already knew who they were because Annie had told him all about them, and he met them once, briefly.

James nodded. "The one who broke your heart."

He was right. "Yes, he's the one."

"Well, he's crazy. From the little I know about his wife, he certainly didn't marry her for her personality." Annie wasn't sure, but she had the feeling James had developed feelings for her. At least, she hoped so because she certainly had for him.

She snickered. "Well, you are right about that. When Will broke up with me for her, I was beyond upset and hurt, not only because I loved him and thought we were going to be married but because she is just so …" She hesitated. She didn't want to be cruel, yet she knew James would understand. "… so horrible." They turned around and made their way back to the farm.

CHAPTER 22

The months seemed to fly by, and once again, winter arrived. Annie couldn't believe it was Christmas morning already, but it was, and she sat up in her bed with a start. All she thought about was that James had told her yesterday that today was going to be a day she would never forget.

Annie had been intrigued by that comment and couldn't wait for his arrival so she could find out what it was all about. He was having dinner with them, and afterward, they would all open gifts.

The ham baked all morning, and while it did, Will, Sam, and Emily arrived, followed shortly by James. Everyone sat around the table talking and laughing and enjoying themselves until Mama announced the meal was ready.

Annie and Beth obediently rose from the table and helped her set out the delicate dishes used only for company and the meal that had everyone's taste buds salivating.

Once everything was in place, Annie took her seat beside James and Pa as the conversation died down and all that was heard was a faint coo from Emily.

Pa rose at the head of the table and cleared his throat. This meant he was about to say grace. Annie always looked forward to Pa's prayers because he made them up so they turned out different every time.

He began. "Dear Heavenly Father, we thank you for this wonderful meal that has been placed before us, and we thank you for the reason we are all gathered together today, the celebration of Your birth. Thank you, Lord, for everything. Amen."

Pa sat down, and everyone else said "Amen" in unison, and then it was time to eat. Each succulent dish was passed around the table until everyone's plates were full. And no one was disappointed with Mama's meal. As always, her food was divine. And Pa said so. "Lily, I don't know how you do it, but each meal is better than the last."

Mama's face flushed. "Thank you, dear."

Will, James, and Beth all followed up with compliments, and Annie knew her mother was pleased. It was important to her that folks enjoy her cooking, which she took great pride in.

After James had eaten about four helpings of potatoes, two slices of ham, and a biscuit, he put down his fork and sat back in his chair. "I am stuffed," he announced. And by that time, everyone else was too.

"Well, I guess nobody wants pie," Mama teased.

"That's not true, Mama," Annie exclaimed. "We're just stuffed right now."

Beth quickly came to her sister's rescue. "We can have pie after we open our gifts," she suggested.

Mama smiled down at her youngest daughter. "I was thinking the same thing."

As soon as the womenfolk cleared the table and washed the dishes, Pa went to the Christmas tree and began handing out gifts. Everyone was so happy with what they received, and after the thank yous had been said, the family sat around the table watching Emily play with the handmade doll given to her by Annie and Beth.

The baby girl sat in Mama's lap with wide-eyed wonder. She looked simply in awe of the Christmas tree and all of the presents.

It disturbed Annie that the precious little girl's mother hadn't held or paid any attention to her the entire evening. As far as Annie could tell, all Sam was interested in was running her fingers through Will's hair and kissing his neck. Annie didn't see why they couldn't keep all of that nuzzling private. After all, she and James were in love, but they weren't broadcasting it.

This last thought reminded her of something. "James?" she enquired.

He turned to her. "What is it, honey?"

He couldn't have forgotten, she thought. "Well, you said there was something you wanted to talk to my pa about."

"Oh," he slapped his forehead in an obviously teasing way. "I had almost forgotten." This had caught everyone's attention, and their curiosity was instantly piqued.

James hesitated, and his face turned white as a sheet. "Out with it, boy," Pa urged.

"W-well, sir, it's actually you that I wanted to have a word with, even though it's not exactly private." James suddenly seemed flustered and looked queasy. Annie was worried it was something serious.

"What is it?" Pa asked. He wasn't sure what this young man was trying to say, but he hoped he would hurry so he wouldn't miss his wife's pie.

With all eyes on him, James addressed Annie's father. "W-well, Mr. Allister," James gulped nervously, "um, as you know, me and Annie have been spending a lot of time together since my family moved here."

Pa nodded his head in agreement. He was well aware. His oldest daughter had scarcely been home in the last few months.

James continued, "Well, in that time, I've grown quite fond of your daughter, and I think she feels the same way about me." He reached his hand up and held hers as she nodded in agreement. "And between helping my father run the mercantile and farmin', I think it's safe to say that I am capable of earnin' a decent living."

He paused, and Pa replied, "I can't argue with you there, boy."

Will sat up straight in his chair, and Annie knew this was the important part. "Well, Mr. Allister, I've given it a great deal of thought, and I know with great certainty that I love Annie enough to ask you for her hand in marriage."

Annie stared at him, stunned. She had absolutely no idea he was planning to do that. But apparently everyone else had seen it coming because Beth jumped out of her chair and threw her arms around her big sister. "It's about time! I'm so happy for you," she cried as tears welled up in her big brown eyes.

"Well," Pa's voice boomed, "I agree with Beth. It's about time you get around to askin' that." He got up and came over to James and began pumping his arm wildly. "You have my blessing."

"Uh, thank you, sir, but first, I need to do this." He bent down on one knee in front of his future bride, took her hand, and asked, "Annie, will you marry me?" He was choked up, and tears welled in his eyes.

And the tears that had filled her eyes moments ago now began to flow. "Of course I will. I love you, James."

"And I love you, darlin'." The couple embraced and shared a brief yet passionate kiss as everyone except Will cheered and clapped. His head was down, almost as though he hadn't even heard what had just happened.

When they were finished, Mama came over to James and gave him a motherly hug. "I am so pleased to have you as a member of our family."

And as she embraced her daughter and congratulated her, she whispered in her ear, "See? I told you you'd find someone to love someday."

"Thank you, Mama," she replied and wiped her eyes with her fingertips. She glanced over at her father who winked approvingly at her.

Sam crawled off her husband's lap and went over to James. "Congratulations, sweetheart," she drawled.

Her voice was full of a sweetness that was obviously fake. She embraced him for longer than necessary and took the opportunity to make one last jab at her cousin by saying, "I don't know what you see in her, but if you ever want a more mature woman, let me know." And she topped off her ridiculous behavior with a kiss to his earlobe.

For a few seconds, everyone in the room was too shocked to say anything. Will's eyes revealed a look of devastation while his cheeks and tips of his ears were bright red with embarrassment. He grabbed her hand. "Sit down, my love," he advised quietly. She sat back down on his lap and gave him a light kiss on his trembling lips.

He tried springing back to normal in the hopes that the others would forget the scene his wife had made. "Now, how about some of that pie that's got my taste buds all excited?" Will piped up. Everyone laughed tensely at that, and Mama, Annie, and Beth served generous slices of delicious apple pie to everyone.

It had been, for the most part, an enjoyable and memorable Christmas, but when little Emily had drifted off to sleep in Mama's arms, Will stifled a yawn. "I suppose Em's trying to tell us something." He grinned.

"Well, that is just great," Sam whined with obvious irritation. "How am I supposed to bundle her without waking her?"

Mama quickly intervened before an argument ensued. "Oh, don't give it another thought. We can make up a bed for her, and she can sleep here for tonight."

"Oh, thank you, Lillian," Will said gratefully. He touched her shoulder gently. "I'll pick her up first thing in the morning."

"You better," Pa teased.

Will chuckled at that. "I will. I promise. Good night, everyone, and thank you for all of the wonderful gifts."

"Come on, William," Sam whined impatiently.

Will knew perfectly well his wife was being rude, and he shot her an irritated look. "Coming, baby." He waved one last time before closing the door behind him.

Soon after, Mama put Emily to bed in the bed she made up for her, and the rest of the family retired shortly after.

And as Annie drifted off to sleep, she couldn't help but think about what had happened. She was still stunned that she was now engaged to be married. She loved James more than anyone or anything.

CHAPTER 23

Four more inches of fresh snow fell in the area two days after Christmas, but that didn't stop James from visiting. He came by every day, sometimes accompanied by his mother. There were wedding plans to be made, and it was important to the couple to involve their families in the plans.

One bright day shortly after the New Year was one of those days, and James, Annie, and their mothers sat around the Allister family table. They were about to discuss the wedding when Will burst in. "The baby's comin'," he panted breathlessly.

Mama jumped up and was on her way to help with the delivery.

Several hours later, she returned home exhausted. By that time, James and his mother had already left, and Beth set a steaming cup of fresh coffee in front of her. "Oh, thank you, honey," Mama said hoarsely.

Beth sat down quickly. "Well, don't keep us in suspense. Is it a boy or a girl?"

Mama sighed. "A baby boy."

"Are Sam and the baby okay?" Annie enquired.

Mama nodded. The sadness was evident in her beautiful blue eyes. "They're fine. They named him Paul William. Or rather, Will named him. And he was also the first to hold the baby." She shook her head slowly. "Sam wouldn't hold him, wouldn't even look at him."

Annie wasn't surprised. She didn't know how her cousin could be so heartless toward her own child.

Mama continued, "I can't understand that girl. It was obvious from the get-go that she didn't want any children. Yet those two are always hanging on each other. Their attraction was purely physical, nothing else. If you ask me, those two should cool it."

But apparently they didn't, because in mid-February, Aunt Frances stormed into the house after visiting her daughter's family. She shouted to anyone who would listen, "That blasted Montgomery boy should be horsewhipped."

Startled, Mama asked, "Frances, what is it?"

The veins in Aunt Frances' forehead looked ready to explode. "She's pregnant."

Mama sighed and put down her sewing. She looked at her sister sternly. She had kept her opinions to herself all this time, but now, she felt she had to say something. "Just don't forget, Frannie, that Sam did her part in making that baby too." Frances said no more, as she didn't know how to respond to that.

Love Will Find a Way

* * *

The wedding plans were almost complete, which was a good thing because spring arrived quickly, and the wedding was scheduled for May 15. Neither Annie nor James attended school any longer. Since they were both sixteen, they already knew the basics and didn't need to return.

It was an unusually warm afternoon in March when Annie was asked to look after Emily and Paul. She happily agreed to it because she loved those children with all her heart. The sun peeked through the clouds when she knocked on the door, and Will answered it almost immediately. Annie instantly noticed a look of sadness in his eyes, which she found odd for a man with this seemingly wonderful life. She would've thought he'd be the happiest man in town.

She stepped inside the house and immediately sensed chaos. The beautiful home her father had helped build was disorderly, as though unattended children occupied it. There were dirty pans on the stove, and a few articles of the children's clothing were strewn about on the floor.

Annie was appalled and hadn't heard Will speaking until he waved a hand in front of her face. "I asked you if you wanted some coffee?"

"Oh, yes. Thank you," she replied. She sat down at the table, and after pouring them both a cup of coffee, Will sat down as well.

He took a quick sip of the lukewarm coffee. "Thank you for helping out today, Annie. It sure does mean a lot."

"Oh, I don't mind one bit." And she meant that. She knew what a lousy housekeeper Sam was, although she would never voice that thought to anyone except James.

Will continued, "I really need to go outside in a bit to get some work done in the barn, and Samantha had riding lessons today."

Annie was caught off guard by that. "Riding lessons?" she asked with raised eyebrows.

Will nodded. "She signed up the minute she met Jack. He's the man who just moved into town and is running the stables."

Annie finished the last of her coffee and set her empty cup down. "Is that safe, in her condition?"

Will shrugged. "Well, she feels cooped up in here all day and wants to get out more."

Annie looked doubtful, which prompted Will to explain further. "Don't worry. I will do my darndest to see that Samantha and the baby are unharmed."

She really hoped Will knew what he was talking about. He noticed her observing the state of the house, and his face turned beet red. "Sorry for the mess. Sam isn't up to keeping house, and I guess I just don't have the touch." He grinned sheepishly.

Annie was appalled that he was the one expected to keep the house clean. "I can clean up a bit," she offered.

Will's eyes widened. "Oh, Annie, thank you. It would sure mean a lot to me."

"It's not a problem."

Will took her hand and gave it a gentle squeeze. "Congratulations, by the way, on your upcoming wedding. James sure is one lucky fella."

Annie blushed. "Well, thank you, but I think I am equally lucky."

They both smiled at each other and continued holding hands. Without warning, Will leaned in and tried to kiss her. His face came so close to her's that she could smell the coffee on his breath. She panicked, knowing it would be wrong to kiss him. She was an engaged woman, and he was a married man. She closed her eyes, preparing for the kiss. What was he doing? And more importantly, what was she thinking? Her mind briefly recalled the love she once felt for him and feared she wouldn't be able to stop him.

Annie was startled when the door flew open with great force. It was Sam making one of her grand entrances. It startled Annie enough to yank her hand away from Will's, although it had been too late. Sam had seen it.

The anger was evident in her beautifully large eyes, which she directed at her cousin. "Get your hands off of my man." Her voice was steady, unfaltering.

Annie tried awkwardly to explain. "I-Sam, I was just ..."

But the gorgeous blond would not let her finish. "You still want him, don't you?" She laughed a wicked laugh. "Well, it's understandable. I mean, that little boy you're marrying doesn't seem like much of a man to me."

Both Annie and Will were in awe of this cold, unfeeling creature standing in front of them. At least now Will would finally know the kind of person his wife really was.

It was almost as if she knew she was on a roll with her unkind remarks because she kept right on going.

"You know, I could probably take him away from you too. It was pure delight seeing your pained expression the day I won William from you. I only married him to get him away from you, and it felt so good when I did."

Annie had heard quite enough. "I'd better go."

"No," Will almost shouted. "Stay." He walked over to his wife. He stared at her ferociously. "How can you be so horrible to another human being? Annie only came over because I asked her to watch the children and nothing more. Have you forgotten I have to work? I needed someone to help out around here, which is more than you seem to do."

The ferocity in Sam's eyes terrified Annie. Sam reached her hand out and slapped Will across the cheek.

Annie was mortified and felt very uncomfortable. She desperately wanted to leave, but she knew Will needed her to stay. Her thoughts were interrupted by the sound of tiny bare feet padding across the floor. She looked over toward the sound and saw Emily emerging from the bedroom. The little girl rubbed her eyes with tiny little fists, and when she sensed the anger in the room, she began to whimper.

She started for the little girl, intending to comfort her, but Sam reached her first and crouched in front of her. But instead of comforting the child, she grabbed her shoulders and shook her firmly. "Shut up this instant, or I will give you a reason to cry." Emily's eyes grew wide with fear, and she stopped crying immediately.

Next, Sam turned to her husband and announced cruelly, "I only stopped by to tell you I will be dining in town tonight with Jack so you will need to feed the children." Then, turning to Annie, she said icily, "Behave yourself with my man." And with that, she turned and flounced out the door, slamming it behind her.

There was an awkward moment of silence before Will's shoulders drooped, and he hung his head in defeat. "I reckon I best get going on that work in the barn." He snuck a quick peek in Annie's direction. "You'll still help?" he asked hopefully, as though he had been disappointed one too many times.

"Of course," she was quick to reassure him. "You go on. I'll take care of things."

He nodded with relief and exited quickly. Annie was glad of that; what she had witnessed between the married couple had been an ugly scene, and she wouldn't have known what to say to Will if he had stuck around.

It was dark by the time Annie returned home. She tiptoed into the house, trying not to wake her sleeping family. Quietly, she made some tea and sat down at the kitchen table.

From the faint glow of the moonlight through the window, she saw Mama emerging from her bedroom. "Hi darlin'," she whispered. "Can't sleep?"

Annie shook her head as Mama poured herself a cup of tea and sat down with it.

"I cooked, played with Emily, ate supper with Will, and cleaned up the house. Now I need some downtime, I guess."

Mama smiled. "Sounds like you got some practice in for when you get married."

But Annie didn't even crack a smile at that, and her mother asked, "What's distracting you, dear?"

Annie looked at her mother with worried eyes. "She is so mean to those children."

It took a moment for Mama to realize the conversation had shifted to the subject of Sam. She brushed it off. "Annie, she's like that with everyone. You know that."

But Annie's eyes held her gaze. "No, Mama," she stressed, "I mean, she is really mean to them, at least with Emily. I saw it with my own two eyes."

That startled her mother. "What do you mean?"

Annie wasn't sure she should tell her mother what she had seen. It was almost as if it hadn't really happened, and saying it out loud would make it true. But it had happened, and she knew she could trust her mother. "She shook Emily. Hard. By the shoulders. And shouted at her."

Mama looked shocked as she shook her head. "It's disgraceful, but unless she harms the child, I'm afraid there's nothing we can do about it. Besides, Will won't let her get out of line with the young'uns."

But Annie was still unconvinced. She stared at the blazing fire in front of her, and when she still hadn't spoken after a few moments, Mama leaned forward in her chair. "Annie? My goodness, I can see you are truly bothered by this. Well, if you feel that strongly about it, I can have a talk with her ma in the morning. Maybe she can straighten out that child of hers."

That made Annie feel somewhat better, and she smiled with relief. "There now," Mama patted her hand, "you'll be able to sleep now, I bet."

"Yes, I think I will." Both women rose from their seats. Annie picked up the empty tea cups and was about to take them to the kitchen when Mama waved a hand in the air. "Just leave them be; I will get them in the morning."

"Alright." They embraced and went to bed, sleeping soundly all night.

CHAPTER 24

The conversation between Mama and Aunt Frances never took place.

Annie sensed something was wrong the second she woke up the next morning. She heard a gruff voice. Dr. Benson? Yes, it was him speaking from the kitchen. She could hear both of her parents too, but they spoke so quietly that their words were barely audible.

She reluctantly threw off her covers and dressed in the frigid darkness of her room. Her eyes were still clouded from sleep, but she managed to wash her face and hands and brush her unruly hair.

When she emerged from her bedroom, Dr. Benson had already left, and Annie wasn't quite prepared for the news she was about to receive.

Her parents sat their two daughters down and told them Aunt Frances had died of a heart attack during the night. She had woken Lillian up, who told Graham to fetch the doctor, but by the time he arrived, Frances had already gone.

Pa and the doctor had taken the body away immediately so the girls wouldn't be upset by it. Afterward, the men came back for some hot coffee before starting the day.

Indeed, it had been a sad day for the family, but as expected, Sam took the news of her mother's passing the hardest. She cried for three days straight, and after the funeral, she began acting out more than ever before.

It was around this time that Will began looking like a defeated old man. His marriage was in jeopardy. Sam was hardly ever home. She spent every waking moment with Jack instead of resting at home protecting her fragile unborn child.

And Will became even more devastated one morning shortly after that when Sam lost the baby. The doctor ordered her to stay in bed for at least a few days, and she took full advantage of it. She made Will fetch things for her all day long.

He sat by her bedside the day after it happened, holding her hand in his. He wrinkled his brow. "Are you okay, darlin'? Do you want to talk about it?"

But Sam appeared unaffected by what she had just endured. In fact, she seemed to have no emotion at all. "Don't be silly, William. I'm fine. Just fetch me some tea, will you?"

But instead of granting his wife's wish, he voiced his fear. "You don't seem too upset that our baby just died."

Suddenly, Sam turned into a ferocious beast, giving her husband an icy look. Her voice was not her own when she spoke. "You know I never wanted another one." And when her husband's silence challenged her to reveal more, Sam gladly rose to it. "If you want me to say it, then yes, I am glad it happened. Now get me that tea."

Will shot his wife an incredulous look. He couldn't believe he had married someone as cold and unfeeling as this monster before him. His head hung in defeat as he rose from his seat.

When he returned a moment later with the tea, she didn't even look at him, but rather motioned to the night stand. He set the tea there and left the room with nothing more to say.

CHAPTER 25

The morning of the wedding arrived quickly and with it came an early morning thunderstorm. The Allister family woke up to loud, booming thunder, intensely bright zig-zags of lightning dancing across the sky, and a downpour of much needed rain.

It quickly passed as the household sat down to a breakfast of pancakes and bacon. And by mid-morning when the family had finished their bathing, the sun was shining, and it promised to be a glorious day.

Annie stopped pacing her bedroom floor long enough to look out her window at the mud puddles that were drying up after the rain. She turned around and looked thoroughly at every square inch of her bedroom. It was a bittersweet day for her, and she would miss this tiny little room terribly. But she was anxious to become Mrs. James Martin as well.

It seemed as though Annie's last day at home with her family flew by, and before she knew it, she stood at the altar of the church with James by her side. The reverend began the ceremony, and it was beautiful. He spoke of the importance of communication between man and wife and how that would help them through rough patches and would most likely ensure a lifelong union.

Annie listened intently, happier than ever. And before she knew it, the reverend had proclaimed them man and wife, they kissed, and were pelted with rice as they ran out of the church toward the only restaurant in town where the celebration was being held.

Their family and friends ate and talked. There was even dancing. James' father was a fiddle player, and he was more than happy to provide the music for the occasion. Annie was still unsure if this was real or not. Was she really a married woman now? It certainly didn't feel real yet. She hadn't even spoken to James all day, except to say "I do," and she felt a tingle rush through her when he suddenly appeared at her side and slid his arm around her slender waist.

She looked up at him with adoration. "It's getting late," he whispered in her ear. "Ready to go home?"

Something about the way he said those last words made Annie love him even more. "Yes," she whispered, and they walked hand in hand past all of their guests and went over to their parents. They said good-bye and hugged them one last time.

The music and party could still be heard as the newly wedded couple descended the rickety steps of the restaurant and made their way to the room above the mercantile, where they would make their home until another could be built.

It was well past sunset, and both the bride and the groom were tired, but Annie's final thought before her magical and highly anticipated wedding night began was that she hoped to have a wonderful and lasting marriage like her parents did. She and James deserved nothing less.

Epilogue

April seemed unusually chilly as it came in with an unexpected snowstorm. The Allister family had had their fair share of tough times, one of them being the situation between Will and Sam. Shortly after Annie's wedding, Sam had run off to the cities with Jack. Apparently, he had persuaded her that he knew people and could get her into showbiz there. Poor gullible Sam believed him, and one morning, she was gone by the time Will woke up. She had left a short note saying her life had not turned out as planned, and she needed to seek out her lifelong dream. She didn't mention her children at all. Sadly, she had abandoned her two precious children and a husband who would move the ends of the earth for her. All for something she didn't even know existed yet.

As terrible as all of that was, it didn't matter to Annie at the moment. She and James had been married for almost a full year now, and she knew it was important to focus on her own life now. She looked down at the tiny bundle cradled in her arms, wrapped in the blue blanket Mama had made in the hopes of a grandson.

And as if her little family wasn't enough to make her gloriously happy, she had also been contacted by the well-known veterinarian of the area. He had known Annie's family since before she was born, and he knew of her aspirations of working with animals and healing them. He was a frail man, and his working days had come to an end. Annie was his first choice to replace him. He would provide all the training she needed to permanently take over for him. She was elated, and since her husband supported the idea, she would begin her career path as soon as she was well enough to do so.

The puzzle pieces of life were all coming together for Annie. She knew there would be plenty of hardships and rough patches along the way, but she would deal with those as they came. For now, she would savor every moment as a wife and new mother today and every day in the future. It was really all that mattered.

END

About the Author

Julie Bentz is an author several years in the making. She is a member of Author Academy Elite. After a tumultuous childhood that consisted of being bullied by her peers, she grew up and started a family. She wrote rough drafts of future books that she hoped would one day become reality. Julie is a single mom of four sons and lives in Rapid City, South Dakota. This is her first novel.

www.ingramcontent.com/pod-product-compliance
Lightning Source LLC
LaVergne TN
LVHW011833060526
838200LV00053B/4006